A
Harlequin
Romance

OTHER
Harlequin Romances
by MARY WIBBERLEY

Many of these titles are available at your local bookseller,
or through the Harlequin Reader Service.

For a free catalogue listing all available Harlequin Romances,
send your name and address to:

HARLEQUIN READER SERVICE,
M.P.O. Box 707, Niagara Falls, N.Y. 14302
Canadian address: Stratford, Ontario, Canada.

or use order coupon at back of book.

THE BENEDICT MAN

by

MARY WIBBERLEY

HARLEQUIN BOOKS   TORONTO
WINNIPEG

Original hard cover edition published in 1974
by Mills & Boon Limited.

© Mary Wibberley 1974

SBN 373-01802-9

Harlequin edition published August 1974

Printed in Canada

CHAPTER ONE

HAD Beth been foolish, giving in her notice so hastily? I wouldn't be the first one to have my illusions shattered, she thought. Perhaps I've been over dramatic. . . . The buzzer sounded, interrupting her thoughts. Quickly she picked up notebook and pencil and went into Mr. Hutchinson's office.

He looked up and gave her a distant nod. "Morning, Miss Kendrick. Mrs. Thornburn wonders if you'd type a couple of letters for her."

"Of course. Good morning, Mrs. Thornburn." Beth turned with a smile to the small plump woman sitting by the window in the office's one easy chair. Her father had founded Associated Chemicals sixty years ago, and she came in to see the boss and his co-director, John Green, every few months on her rare visits to London. Beth had the greatest affection for her because she radiated an air of good humour, and was unfailingly cheerful despite an arthritic hip that must have cost her a great deal of pain. She would have typed a hundred letters for Mrs. Thornburn if she had asked her.

Mr. Hutchinson stood up and cleared his throat pompously.

"If you'll excuse me, I'll go and attend to some matters while you're doing the letters." He looked at his watch, then at Beth, and went out. He wasn't pleased that Beth was leaving, she knew, and managed to express it in lots of ways. She gave a small sigh and sat down opposite the old lady, who then began to dictate slowly and clearly in her beautiful voice.

When she had finished, Beth stood up. "I'll do them right away, but first I'll bring you a cup of coffee. Black, with two sugars, isn't it?"

She chuckled. "Bless you, you do look after me, dear. I enjoy seeing you when I come here. You're like a breath of fresh air in these stuffy offices."

"I'm afraid I won't be here much longer, Mrs. Thornburn. I'm leaving next weekend," Beth answered. "I was going to say goodbye when you went today, for I don't imagine you'll be here again before I go."

Her eyes widened, and she looked up sharply. "Leaving? My dear child, surely not? You've always seemed so happy here, and I thought – forgive me – but aren't you practically engaged to Green's son Alan?"

A warm tide of colour swept up Beth's face as she shook her head.

"I was. I – I'm not now."

Mrs. Thornburn put out her hand in a placatory gesture. "Sorry, my dear. I'm a nosey old woman. I shouldn't have asked. But please, just tell me one thing. Have you a good job to go to?"

"No. I gave in my notice on impulse. I mean to have a couple of weeks at home with my mother, then look around. I'd like to get away from London, I think." Beth wondered why she added that.

She nodded thoughtfully. "Yes, you won't have much trouble, with your abilities." Then she looked keenly at the girl before her and it seemed that she was about to say something else. Before she could speak, Mr. Hutchinson came in, smoothing back his sparse grey hair self-consciously. "That's that sorted out. Trouble in the packing room again. Well –" his eyes flickered over Beth's notebook. "Before you type those out, Miss Kendrick, perhaps you'll bring coffee for us both?"

"I was just going to do so, sir." She smiled at Mrs. Thornburn and went out. Returning with the coffee a few minutes later, she handed it to them and was about to leave, when the old lady's voice stopped her.

"Just a moment, Miss Kendrick."

"Yes, Mrs. Thornburn?" Beth waited, hand on door.

"Will you do me a favour?"

She smiled. "Of course, if I can."

"Then have lunch with me. I want to talk with you." She turned to the waiting man. "Will you let her have an extra half-hour?"

He inclined his head slightly, a stiff little smile at his mouth. "How can I refuse you, Miss Thornburn?"

And so it was arranged. Beth was pleased by the invitation, but she was also puzzled.

The lunch was superb. Used as Beth was to beans on toast, or a quick ham sandwich before dashing round the shops, the duckling à l'orange served at the hotel round the corner from the office was a delightful contrast, and she told her hostess so. She laughed, carefully spearing a sliver of Gruyère cheese before saying: "Well now, we'll order coffee, I think. Then to business."

7

"Business?" Beth echoed faintly. All through the meal Mrs. Thornburn had kept up a flow of fascinating conversation about anything and everything – but never a word of her reason for the sudden, surprising invitation to lunch. Now she was about to find out.

Beth poured coffee into the fragile china, and the old lady nodded approvingly. "Good and strong and black. Now, my dear, I don't believe in beating about the bush, so I'll tell you why I've asked you to come here. Quite simply, it's this. I need a secretary-companion. I've seen your work, and I admire your neatness and efficiency." Her faded blue eyes lighted momentarily. "I also like the pleasant smile you always have for me. So, as you're leaving Associated Chemicals, and I won't be stealing you, I'm asking you to consider my offer. You won't regret it financially, I promise you."

Beth put her cup down carefully. She supposed that she had half suspected this from the time when Mrs. Thornburn had first asked her to lunch, but to actually hear the words was a shock. She looked across the table, and the eyes of the two women met in a glance of complete frankness.

"I'm very honoured to think you'd like me to work for you," Beth began hesitantly. "And it's rather a surprise, I must admit. You live so far away, don't you? Up north, I mean?"

She gave her low familiar chuckle. "Heavens, child, you make it sound like the frozen wilds! I live in Derbyshire, and it's only a couple of hours by train from here – and you did say you wanted to leave London."

Beth nodded, smiling ruefully. "I know. Forgive me

for seeming rude. I'm just startled, that's all."

Mrs. Thornburn patted her hand briskly with her own heavily beringed one. The soft gleam of a huge amethyst caught the light, and Beth watched it fascinated.

"Will you promise to think it over?"

"Yes, I will. I'd like to talk to my mother tonight. She's a widow, you see, and there's only my young sister at home with her."

"Then you must, of course. I'm staying at the Fitz-william Hotel overnight, but I'll be going back home tomorrow lunchtime with my nephew to Benedict House. You can phone me until about eleven tonight, or before noon tomorrow."

"I will, and thank you for asking me."

She shook her head briskly. "Nonsense. I know a good worker when I see one. Now, off you go, back to your desk. I'll stay here a while, and have another coffee. Goodbye, my dear – and don't let me down."

Beth smiled. "Goodbye, Mrs. Thornburn. And thank you for a lovely lunch."

The motion of the train had a soothing effect. Beth had bought several paperbacks and magazines at Euston, and had a sticky bar of chocolate pressed into her hand by Judith, her sister, before she had left. Strangely, it was she who had been appalled at the idea of Beth taking a job in the wilds. Her mother had been delighted, but then she had never liked Alan, never been able to see why Beth had fallen for him. And as the miles slipped past, Beth realised something else about her. She was still young, and her leaving home had given her

9

mother the incentive to go out and get herself a job. Meeting people would do her good, shake her out of the lethargy into which she had sunk after losing her husband, Beth and Judith's father, three years previously. Judith, a tall, leggy teenager of nearly sixteen, was becoming daily more independent, with her own circle of friends. She could start life anew, perhaps even get married. . . . Beth gazed dreamily out of the window at the darkening countryside rushing past. Another hour before they reached Derby, and then she had to change to a branch line which would take her to Appledore. Her reflection looked back at her through the darkened glass, a little apprehensive perhaps. But then she had never been to Derbyshire before, and in her complete ignorance had imagined it to be bleak and grim. She pulled her hair back tightly into a chignon for the journey, and it gleamed palely in the overhead light; her face was partly in shadow, but her eyes seemed larger, and darker, than usual. A trick of the light, undoubtedly, but she looked almost timid at that moment. Beth smiled to herself and turned away, and her eye was caught by that of a young man across the carriage, sitting with his girl. Just for a moment he reminded her of Alan, and her heart lurched oddly.

It wasn't so easy to forget him, after all. She was better away from London, still better away from Associated Chemicals, working every day for his father's partner, and wondering why it had taken her so long to find out that Alan's world and hers were poles apart.

She'd worked there a year before chance took her from the typing pool and into Mr. Hutchinson's office.

He had liked the occasional work she had done for him, and when his secretary left to have a baby, Beth had got the job. Alan had come into the office one day, a tall good-looking blond giant, looking for his father. He had made some trivial remark – but Beth had seen the spark of admiration in his eyes, and responded like any other normal female, when he had asked her out. The friendship had survived the usual nine days' wonder of office gossip, and had developed into something warmer. At nineteen Beth had been too young, too blind, to see what must have been so obvious to her mother. She was in love with love. Alan was charming and well mannered. He drove a super sports car, and they went around with a crowd she didn't particularly like, but because they were his friends, she had tried to. To them, Beth supposed she was a novelty. A schoolteacher's daughter who actually had to work for a living! She looked down quickly at the magazine on the table in front of her, unable to keep the bitterness from her face. How stupid she had been! Nobody had ever dared to be patronising, because Alan had a sharp edge to his tongue when he wanted, but Beth knew she wasn't one of them.

Just how different their lives were she didn't fully realise until only recently. Alan had asked her down for the weekend to his aunt's home, in a little village in Sussex. Beth suspected nothing, the invitation was all open and above board. He had said casually, when he had asked her, "I say, don't mention this to the old man, will you? He's never got on with Auntie Cissie, doesn't care for me visiting her." Beth had thought nothing of it. His family were always feuding with someone, so it seemed quite normal. They set off late on Friday evening in his car, and arrived about eleven at the little village near Battle. It was only when she saw the cottage was in darkness that Beth began to feel uneasy. Surely there would be lights if his aunt was expecting them? When he opened the door with a key, Beth had said something like, "How did you get that?" and he had answered, "Oh, I always have one." Inside, everything was neat and spruce, and clearly unlived in.

She looked at him as he put down the cases, and seeing the expression in his eyes, went cold. "She's not here, is she?" Beth asked.

He gave a boyish grin. "Well, actually, no – but listen –" this as she made for her suitcase. "Beth, look, let's have a drink. Don't be mad at me. You know how I feel about you. God knows, I'm not made of stone."

"Why – why this way?" she said. "How could you?"

He held up his hands. "All right, I'm sorry. I was sly about it. I might as well own up, because you've got a dreadful gleam in your eyes. I was going to pretend to be very surprised at her being out when we got here, and tell you she'd be back any minute, and meanwhile we'd just have a drink, and . . ." he flung his hands up, "but – well, all right, she's abroad if you must know. I knew damn well the place would be empty – so go ahead. Shoot me!"

Beth shook her head. "I was a fool to come. Anyway, I'm not stopping here. You can if you like. Where's the local pub?"

He took her arm. "You can't go there now. It's nearly twelve. They'll be all bolted and barred and abed. Relax, Beth. Look, let's have a cup of coffee, and talk things over."

"There's nothing to talk over," she said wearily. She was shocked at her own reaction. She didn't even feel horrified, or frightened; merely a huge, yawning indifference. She was fond of Alan, had even thought herself to be in love with him. And now, when he had manoeuvred her into a cottage in the country with the intention of seducing her, all Beth wanted to do was go to bed with a hot water bottle and a book. She knew then that it was all over. Not because she was a prude, but because the gulf between them, so imperceptibly growing, had at last yawned wide open, and all the tiny irritations, all the things she had ignored, or pretended to, came rushing forward, and she saw him at last for what he was – shallow, pleasure-seeking, living only for the moment. He still hoped to talk her into sleeping with him. Well, Beth thought, as she made coffee in the chintzy, olde-worlde kitchen, you're in for a shock, my friend.

The next morning they left the cottage to go home. As they walked down the path, a man with a dog appeared through the trees in the lane ahead and paused slightly, looking at them both, before saying:

"Good morning."

Alan answered him, the man walked on, and then, as they got into the car, Beth saw that Alan was quite pale.

"What's the matter?" she asked.

He looked at her. "Fancy seeing him, of all people!" he muttered.

"Why? Who was it?" Beth turned round and stared

at the stranger's retreating back. He was tall and well built, and he walked with an easy grace that implied that he didn't give a damn for anyone. His face was imprinted on her mind, tanned, a wide well-shaped mouth; black hair and sideburns. He had grinned when he had seen them, only slightly, but it was a knowing grin, and she realised, suddenly, exactly what the man was thinking. The grey eyes under black, level brows had been amused too. Beth turned away.

"Who is he?" she asked dully.

"He's – no, it doesn't matter." Alan glanced bitterly at me. "And to think he imagines – my God! he couldn't be more wrong, could he?" And he started the car with a jerk and a grating of gears, and they went home.

Beth came back to the present with a start, shivering slightly, for the train had gone cooler. She couldn't forget that stranger's face, and as she remembered it, the amusement in those grey eyes seemed to turn to contempt as they surveyed them. He was entitled to his thoughts, yet suddenly Beth wished it had been possible to have told him that she had slept alone, behind a locked door, the previous night. And Alan had never told her who he was. They had hardly spoken on the way home. His pride was badly dented, and she was responsible.

It was no surprise to see him out, a few days later, with Ellen Peters, a stunning red-head member of his circle. It hurt terribly, but it helped Beth decide what she must do. The following day she gave in her notice, and held her head up high, ignoring the knowing remarks that came her way. Alan went off to America for

14

a month on a selling trip with three other senior sales-men. When he came back Beth would be gone. And she didn't intend to see him again.

It was dark when Beth stepped off the train at Apple-dore, the only one to alight. She looked round her in dismay, wondering for a moment if she'd mistaken the situation. Not a soul was about. The train began to move and she watched it go, much, she supposed, as a drown-ing man sees his ship slowly sailing away, out of sight, in a vast ocean. There was a sharp nip in the air, and she repressed a shiver. Silver points dotted the dark sky, they twinkled and shone, and the air smelt fresh and cold.

A gas light flickered and nearly went out as she picked up her two cases and began to walk to the station-master's office. Mrs. Thornburn had assured her that someone would meet her, when she had written, but per-haps, if the train was in early, they would still be on their way. The black shadow that detached itself from the wall just outside the stationmaster's office made her jump, and a dark rich brown voice said:

"Miss Kendrick, I presume?"

"Yes." Beth peered through the gloom at him. "Were you here all the time? I couldn't see a soul."

He laughed as he came forward into the light, and she saw a young man, good-looking in a fine-boned way, with dark hair.

"Guilty as charged. I had the urge to see Aunt Lavi-nia's new sec, so I stood and peeped, I admit it."

He had a refreshing manner about him that made her

laugh, and he gave an approving nod. "That's it. You've got a sense of humour, thank God. Not like the last one." He took the cases from her, and added, "I'm Giles Benedict."

"Oh! You must be Mrs. Thornburn's nephew."

He laughed. "Well – yes, I am. But I'm not the one you think. I don't live at Benedict House."

"Oh, I see." She didn't, but it wasn't important at that moment, for she was tired, and cold, and hungry.

"This way, Miss Kendrick." He strode off into the darkness, and Beth hastened after him before he could vanish entirely. The place was so quiet, she had the awful feeling that if she let him out of sight, she'd never see another human being again. Outside, lit only dimly by the solitary flickering gas lamp on the wall, was a sports car. He opened the boot and put her luggage in, then opened the passenger door.

They roared away from the station, and Beth turned back for a last glimpse. "I didn't see a soul. Is it always like that?" she asked.

He slowed slightly to negotiate a sharp bend, and then turned a laughing face towards her. "You're in the wilds now. Didn't Aunt Lavinia prepare you?"

She shook her head, smiling a little. "It sounds silly, but I've never been to Derbyshire before."

"Hmm? You haven't lived, have you? Never been to Derbyshire indeed!" Something in the way he said it made her glance quickly at him, and he caught the look and smiled wryly. "Does it show?"

"You don't like it?"

"Well, not exactly. But it's so quiet here. Especially

16

in winter." His tone changed suddenly. "I'll tell you something, though. I've got a weakness for beautiful slim blondes – I might stick around, instead of joining the French Foreign Legion, as I was about to do just before you came into my life."

The outrageous compliment made her laugh, and he groaned. "Don't do that! Do you want me to crash? What colour are your eyes?"

"Blue." Beth added, "And don't you think it's time you concentrated –"

"– on my driving? Yes. And anyway, we're here." So saying, he turned into a gateway, missing the high stone posts by inches, and they began to go up a wide gravelled drive. Beth could see nothing for the thick trees and the darkness surrounding them, and her heart bumped erratically. She was about to see Benedict House for the first time. What would it be like? Country houses had always fascinated her, and she hoped that this wouldn't be some Victorian monstrosity . . . She drew in her breath sharply as they came round a curve and it was there, before them. Giles heard her gasp, and said softly: "You like it?"

"Oh, yes." Beth's voice was barely a whisper. "It's beautiful." And it was. Even though it was night, she could see the well proportioned lines of the large, ivy-smothered stone building in front of them, lit in nearly every room, so that warm light spilled out of the tall elegant windows in a blaze of gold. She caught her breath as they drew slowly nearer. She wanted very much to see it in daylight.

Giles said quietly, "It always hits people suddenly.

I'm pleased that you like it. I'd have been disappointed if you hadn't."

Beth looked at him. For the first time since they'd met, he was serious. She decided she liked him, very much.

The door was opened as she got out of the car. She looked up to see Mrs. Thornburn standing in the entrance, leaning slightly on her cane, her other hand held out in a welcoming gesture.

"My dear Miss Kendrick! Welcome to Benedict House."

For one absurd moment, as Beth ran up the steps to greet her, she felt as if she was coming home. The sensation passed in a moment as she had her first impression of the light and warmth of the vast hall in which they stood. A log fire burned to the left, and the reflections from the flames were caught and held in the chandeliers that swayed slightly in the draught from the open door. Giles came in with the cases, and gave an exaggerated shiver. "Brr! Cold outside. Well, Aunt, I'll be away now." He crossed to her, and gave her an affectionate peck on the cheek. "And don't make her work too hard, hey?" He winked at Beth. "We don't want to frighten Miss Kendrick away — not until I've got to know her better, anyway."

His aunt laughed. "Now that's enough, Giles." There was strong affection in the light tap she gave him. "Thank you for meeting Miss Kendrick. You're a good boy, sometimes."

After he had gone, she said: "He's a lovely boy, is Giles. Just remember to take everything he tells you with a pinch of salt, and you'll not go far wrong. Well, my dear, how did the journey go? I have a meal ready for you, but first –" she pressed a bell at the side of the fireplace, and Beth heard a distant buzz, "I'll get Mrs. Macdonald to show you to your room. When you're ready, come down. I'll be in there." She pointed to a doorway. "We'll have a talk about things. There's quite a lot I must tell you."

"Thank you. I won't be long," Beth promised. She was curious. Something in Mrs. Thornburn's tone reminded her of the time in the office when she had asked Beth to have lunch with her, some holding back of a secret.

Mrs. Macdonald was tall and dark-haired, and in her forties, Beth imagined. She seemed shy, for she spoke little as she led the way upstairs. Yet her smile was warm as Beth looked round the modern well furnished bedroom, then she said quietly:

"It's different up here, miss, isn't it?"

Beth looked at her, caught the gleam of pride that shone in her eyes, and gave an answering smile. "It's so modern," she replied in surprise. "I expected something different."

Beth's eyes took in the white walls, the picture beside her bed of a fishing harbour at night, muted browns and greys, fascinating; and the blonde wood furniture, new, yet blending in so perfectly with everything.

"Mr. Benedict likes to keep the downstairs rooms in character with the house, but up here it's like a different place." She went over and closed the pale lemon curtains with a soft swish. "Your meal's ready, miss.

Your bathroom is the door before this. You'll have it to yourself, for Mrs. Thornburn and Mr. Benedict have their own." And with that Mrs. Macdonald went out, shutting the door quietly after her. Beth was left with the impression that she was a woman of strong personality, yet quiet dignity. She wondered who else she was to encounter at Benedict House.

Later, sitting in the comfortable lounge, drinking coffee and Tia Maria with her new employer, Beth found out what her duties were to be.

"You did say you could drive, didn't you, Miss Kendrick?" Mrs. Thornburn asked, sitting herself more comfortably beside Beth on the lush cushions of a burgundy velvet settee that she had the greatest difficulty in keeping awake on.

"Yes, I did – and please call me Beth. But I've not done a lot of driving."

"No? Well, there's not much traffic around here – except at weekends, and I rarely go out then anyway, unless David persuades me. Beth – yes, I will call you Beth. It's very kind of you, and do you know, it suits you so well? So slim and fair, with those blue eyes. Dear me, I think Giles was quite taken with you. How old are you, Beth? Or is that a very rude question for a nosey old woman like me to ask?"

She smiled. "Of course not. I'm almost twenty. May I ask you a question, please? Giles said something about him 'not being the nephew I thought' and I didn't know what he meant – but now you've mentioned someone called David. Is he another one?"

20

Mrs. Thornburn clasped her hands over her ample bosom. "There now! I'm confusing you, aren't I? You must say if I do. I get quite forgetful sometimes — now, where was I? Oh, yes. I had two younger brothers, John and Robert, both now dead. Giles is Robert's son. He's twenty-six, and lives with his mother about two miles away in a Georgian house. It's charming, but you'll see for yourself soon. I sometimes visit them." She paused, then gave her deep chuckle. "And David — well, there I've got a slight confession to make. David is John's son. The house is his, although it's been my home since my husband died twelve years ago, and will be, I hope, until I die." Beth nodded politely. What on earth could the confession be? she wondered.

"I see," Beth said. "And is he here now?"

"No. Otherwise I'm quite sure he'd have met you — though as a matter of fact —" she paused and twisted a huge topaz ring round her finger, watching it intently as she continued "— I haven't told him that you're coming yet, so in a way I'm quite pleased he had to go away to Paris for a few days. He'll be back tomorrow night."

Beth went cold. Surely Mrs. Thornburn wasn't going to spring her on this David person on his return? "Oh, I say, I've hired a secretary companion, hope you don't mind." Her thoughts must have shown on her face as she looked at her employer, for she suddenly began to laugh in her deep, infectious way. "Oh, heavens, it's not like that! He's not an ogre. It's just —" she stopped, and took a deep breath. "I'm being a silly old woman, aren't I? Well, David is a writer. He needs a secretary

21

more than I do, though, heaven knows, I'm on enough committees and things, but it won't be a full-time job, you working for me, so I wondered if you'd – well, put in a couple of days a week for him. Er – can you type scripts?"

So that was it! Beth heaved a sigh of relief. "Why, yes. You had me worried for a moment. Of course I will." A thought struck her. "Scripts, did you say? Well, I did a few for a play at Judith's school last year, but I'm not really an expert – does he write plays?"

Mrs. Thornburn beamed happily. "That'll do. You know the ropes. Then you don't mind? Good. Yes, he does several things for television," she dismissed them with an airy wave of her hand. "The sort of thing that I, quite frankly, can't watch, though I wouldn't hurt his feelings for the world, of course. He's a dear boy, and it seems to keep him busy, though – I don't know," she gave a sad sigh. "It does seem a shame he's not interested in the business. He just won't have anything to do with it. All he wants to do is write." Her eyebrows arched, faintly surprised, as she added: "I don't mind, of course, and it's none of my business, but it's really not a job for a man."

Beth had to smile at her tone, but as in all fairness she couldn't pass comment, she merely said: "I've heard that television pays well, so perhaps –"

"Oh, it's not the *money*!" She sounded faintly horrified. "If it was, it wouldn't be so bad. It just doesn't seem quite nice, if you know what I mean."

It seemed time to change the subject, which Beth did

by admiring some delightful miniatures at the side of the fireplace. A picture of the absent nephew was forcing itself into her mind. A trendy, slightly effeminate version of Giles was the unfortunate vision that refused to go away, and a feeling of dismay came with it. And what sort of things did he write if his aunt couldn't watch? Her mind boggled at the dire possibilities. Fortunately, he wasn't mentioned again, and soon afterwards they bade each other goodnight. It was nearly midnight, Sunday. In the morning at nine o'clock, Beth officially started her new job. As she closed her bedroom door behind her, she made a fervent wish that she wouldn't disappoint Mrs. Thornburn. She had given her the chance to begin a new life, and to forget Alan.

Beth had had some indication of the charity work done by her new employer when she had typed letters for her at Associated Chemicals, and went down to breakfast the following morning, ready to start immediately afterwards, her notebook and pencil at the ready. She had brought her portable typewriter, although it was fair to assume there was already one in the house. Mrs. Macdonald was hovering in the hall, and said immediately: "Good morning, Miss Kendrick. Mrs. Thornburn hopes you'll excuse her this once. She had a bad night's sleep and will see you after breakfast. If you'll follow me, I'll take you to the dining room."

When Beth had eaten, she went to the window and had her first look at the gardens and countryside surrounding Benedict House. She wanted to see whether her preconceived ideas were right. Immediately outside

23

the big window, with its deep embrasure, was a gravel path, then the lawn began, rich and dark green, with well laid out rose beds, the roses still blooming, although it was nearly October. Shrubs and bushes were dotted about, with further away tall cypresses, elegant sentries guarding the stone house, and leading the eye easily on still further towards huge oaks and elms that had clearly stood undisturbed for centuries.

She looked and looked, fascinated, drinking it all in, the shading and merging of the different greens against the brilliant contrast of the red roses, and she knew that she had to go out as soon as she could, and explore it properly. For a moment her heart was filled with a bursting happiness that was almost pain. Beth had been apprehensive, wondering what she was coming to, and now she knew, and the beauty overwhelmed her.

"I see you're admiring the roses."

Beth turned to see Mrs. Thornburn coming in the door, and moved to assist her. "No, no, I can manage, my dear. Just a few twinges in the night, that's all. I'm a silly old woman. You can go and walk round the gardens this afternoon. I certainly don't intend to overwork you on your first day here. I'd have let you go this morning, but there are a few letters I must get to post, and the laundry man will take them when he comes at noon." She sat down heavily on a chair by the table, and passed Beth her stick. "There now, a cup of coffee would be nice, I think. You'll have another?"

"Certainly." Beth poured two out, and handed her one. "Is there any particular room we'll work in, Mrs. Thornburn?"

She laughed. "Do I have a study, do you mean? No. David does, and heaven help anyone who goes in! But I prefer the drawing room, or the library on a sunny day – yes, we'll try the library this morning. You get a splendid view of the hills from there, and it traps all the sun."

The morning passed swiftly. Beth scarcely noticed the girl who brought in the mid-morning coffee, so busy and engrossed was she in a pile of letters. Only Mrs. Thornburn's comment: "That's Mrs. Macdonald's daughter, Anne," brought her back to the present. She seemed to be watching, waiting for an opinion, so Beth admitted that she hadn't noticed her.

"Personally, I consider the girl's wasted here. She had a brilliant brain – but she doesn't seem to want to leave her mother."

"How old is she?" Beth asked.

"About your age, or a bit younger. And pretty too, in a dark way. Ah well!" she gave a brisk nod. "This won't do, will it? I mustn't gossip the morning away. Tell me, will that typewriter do for you? And you've found all the paper and envelopes in that top drawer? Good. Then I'll leave you to get on with it, and go and see about lunch."

Dressed in a warm coat Beth set off after lunch to explore the grounds. They extended for miles, so Mrs. Thornburn had assured her, but only the gardens round the house were tended and cultivated. The invisible demarcation line began past the cypresses, and there, she said, she would see rabbits and squirrels. She drew a rough map of the area surrounding the house, marking a lake where herons were occasionally seen. And as they parted at the door, she handed Beth a huge pair of binoculars, which she slung round her neck. "There now. Off you go, my dear. Don't lose your way!"

"I won't. And thank you for letting me have the afternoon off. You're quite sure –?"

"Quite sure. David will be back this evening, and we want a good dinner ready. Mrs. Macdonald and I will have to have a talk about it. She enjoys trying out exciting new dishes for him. He really appreciates good food, and after Paris – well!" Her hands went up in a gesture that implied that the heavens would descend if the dinner wasn't absolutely perfect. With a smile and a farewell Beth set off, but inside she felt the flutters of doubt again. There was always a fly in the ointment. Mrs. Thornburn idolised her nephew. There was affection in every word when she spoke of him. He would be slim, and rather pale, Beth decided. Long hair, possibly bearded; a lot of writers were, and somewhere in his thirties. He would definitely wear outlandish clothes. Purple shirts, sandals. . . . Beth shook herself irritably. Why spoil an enjoyable stroll by worrying about her new part-time employer? He might, heaven knows, be quite pleasant and agreeable. Giles was. There was no earthly reason to suppose that his cousin would be any different. She looked around her, and stopped, forgetting David Benedict in an instant of wonderment at what lay before her. She must have strayed from the path, and ahead of her was a large expanse of water, surrounded by trees and rhododendron bushes.

Beyond stretched more trees, almost a wood, and only distantly could she see the hills, the grey guardian Pennines, stretching in a long line for miles. She put the binoculars to her eyes, and everything sprang to life with the intense magnification. Turning, she could barely see the house, so thickly wooded was the land. She gave a deep contented sigh. To think she had imagined this to be grim! Rugged, yes, but with a beauty of its own that surrounded and filled Beth with a sense of timelessness, and belonging. The air was so fresh and cold that it almost hurt, and she smiled wryly, remembering how she had slept the previous night, her first. She had expected to lie awake for ages, as she always did in a strange bed, but instead she had been away the moment her head had touched the pillow. So this was Derbyshire. And she had doubted, wondering if she was doing the right thing. Now she knew.

It was time to start back. Beth had been away over an hour. There would be plenty more days for country walks, plenty of time to see it all and appreciate the country more fully. She turned round, and started retracing her steps.

She was thinking fondly of a cup of tea as she reached the garages at the back of the house. So huge and dark, a long low stone building, curiosity impelled her to stop, and hesitating a little, look inside. She was more than a little interested to know what car she might have to drive. Surely not a huge Daimler, or a Bentley? The thought made her giggle as she made out the lines of a large car just inside the first, open door – and then she heard a noise, and a man stepped from the furthest recesses of the huge building, wiping his hands on an oily rag.

Beth could scarcely see him, for a spot lamp was on directly behind him, only that he was tall and broad, and was walking towards her in a vaguely familiar way. Then suddenly he spoke, his voice polite but discouraging.

"Good afternoon. Can I help you?" As he said the words, he came nearer, and she saw him then, properly. She looked up into slate grey eyes, and experienced a shock of recognition. This was the man whose face she had been unable to forget; the man who had greeted them outside Alan's cottage on that disastrous, unforgettable visit.

CHAPTER TWO

Beth managed to find her voice eventually, although her mind still wrestled with the shock. "Thank you. I was just admiring the car. I – I work for Mrs. Thornburn."

"I see." But it seemed as if he frowned slightly. Beth wondered, in one terrible moment, if he recognised her. Surely not – he had only had a glimpse. Yet his face was imprinted on her mind.

She wanted, suddenly, to escape, to go back to the house. It was possible that he was a friend of Giles', though why he should be here, she couldn't imagine. The memory of the mocking look he had given them outside the cottage was so strong that Beth instinctively turned away before she betrayed herself. Perhaps he would be gone, like a bad dream, before dinner time.

"Just a moment. You work for Mrs. Thornburn, you say? Then I imagine you only started today?" His voice was hard, questioning.

"Yes. Excuse me, I'd better go in."

"First I'd better introduce myself, although I'm sure my aunt would rather do it in style, when I'm a bit more presentable. I'm David Benedict." He held out his hand, and, mesmerised, Beth took it.

"I – my name's Beth Kendrick." His grip was strong and firm. "I thought you were in Paris," she blurted out foolishly.

"I was. I caught an earlier plane back because of fog

warnings. I imagine I'll see you later, Miss Kendrick. Goodbye." He nodded briefly and went back to the depths of the garage. Beth walked away quickly towards the house and ran up the front steps, seeing nothing, numb with shock.

Safely in her bedroom, she sat at the dressing table and looked at herself in the mirror. Almost automatically she picked up the brush and began sweeping her hair back. It had been loose, that other, dreadful morning. In future, she would wear it in a chignon. For some reason she couldn't put words to, Beth didn't want him to recognise her. Yet she didn't know why the thought should be so distressing. She knew that nothing had happened at the cottage. She could hold her head up high, and not give a damn for anyone – just as David Benedict appeared to do. She blotted her lipstick, picked up the binoculars, and went downstairs.

Beth found Mrs. Thornburn in the room where they had sat the previous evening. It was clearly her favourite. Books and magazines were scattered round her on the settee, some knitting had fallen to the floor, and she sat comfortably back, her feet on a footstool, eyes closed. Just as Beth was about to creep out again, she woke and stretched herself.

"Ah, dear me, I must have dozed –" she looked round distractedly and Beth bent to pick up the knitting.

"I'm sorry if I disturbed you. Is this what you want?"

"Ah, yes, my dear. Thank you. You know, I'm a hopeless knitter really, but I enjoy doing these." She pointed to the cushion beside her and Beth saw several multi-coloured pieces of knitting, about eight inches square. "I pass them on to the Women's Institute, and someone crochets them into blankets for old people." She smiled proudly. "I don't feel so completely useless then, you see."

"You, useless?" Beth had to smile at that. "I'm sure that's the last thing anyone could accuse you of."

"Hmm, you do say nice things, Beth. But when one gets past seventy, one realises –" she stopped abruptly as the door opened and David Benedict walked in. "David! My dear! But why back so early? I thought –" He went across towards her, and Beth watched him, heart in mouth. Seen now, in the lighted room, he was devastatingly attractive. There are those who have only to walk into a crowded room and everything stops, all eyes riveted to them. So Beth felt it was with this man. He wore a brown suede jacket, with matching slacks. Tall, lean, broad-shouldered, he moved with an easy grace that belied his size as he leaned over to kiss his aunt on the cheek. Then he turned and looked directly at Beth.

She met his glance coolly, with a slight smile. All good-looking men are conceited, she thought, and she had no intention of letting him see she found him overwhelming. Yet inside, she was in a turmoil. There was a grey cynicism about his eyes that was fascinating, as if he didn't care about his looks – more, as if everything was slightly off balance – except him. The dark thick brows contracted as he frowned slightly. Was this the moment? Beth went cold. Was he going to say it now? 'Didn't I see you a few weeks ago at. . . .' But nothing like that. Instead: "Well, Aunt, Miss Kendrick tells me she's working for you."

His aunt's face crumpled in dismay. "Oh, you've met?"

He gave a slight smile. "Yes. Outside the garage. I think Miss Kendrick thought she'd have to drive the old Rolls. I found her looking at it slightly shocked."

"Oh, dear, no." His aunt began to laugh. "I've a smaller one, a Rover. You should have shown her, David." She gave him a reproachful look.

"I would have done, but I didn't have time. My car was playing up all the way from Manchester Airport – and Miss Kendrick seemed in a hurry to get back to you." He shrugged, and then looked at Beth. She found it an oddly disturbing glance, dark and unsmiling. "However, any time you wish to look round, just tell me."

"Thank you, Mr. Benedict." Beth managed to smile, subduing the flutter of apprehension that would not be stilled.

He looked at his watch, then at the mantel clock. "That thing's slow again. Well, I'm off to do some work. Don't wait dinner for me, Mrs. Macdonald can bring me a bite later."

"But, David!" His aunt's dismayed voice stopped him in his tracks. He turned slowly, almost irritably. "I've got her to make some of your favourite – the ratatouille, with peach meringue to follow."

"Dear Aunt, I wish you wouldn't." He shook his head resignedly, and Beth felt a stab of dislike pierce her. If only he knew what trouble Mrs. Thornburn had been to to make sure his homecoming meal for her beloved nephew was just perfect. But he didn't care.

She gave a little laugh, but it didn't fool Beth. "Oh, well, never mind, I know your writing's important, and I'm sure that Beth and I will enjoy it, eh, my dear?"

"It sounds wonderful," Beth agreed as she watched him stride out, shutting the door firmly behind him.

She didn't see him again that evening. Long after Beth had gone to bed that night, unable to sleep, she went to the window to draw back the curtains. Her room was at the back, in a jutting out wing of the 'E'-shaped building. Down below, in the room next to the library, a light burned, the only one for miles around. Everything else slept.

The following morning, Beth drove Mrs. Thornburn to Buxton, twelve miles away, to do some shopping. At first she was nervous, driving the comparatively large car – she had learnt in a Morris Minor – but the roads were quiet, and gradually she relaxed. For once her normally garrulous employer was quiet. It was only as she directed Beth into a car park at the end of the town that she spoke.

"There now, it wasn't so bad, was it?"

"You knew?" Beth looked at her in surprise as she put the ignition key safely in her bag.

"I could tell you were nervous when we set off, but I knew you'd find your feet after a few miles. Tuesdays are quiet here on the roads. It's only on Saturdays and Sundays I avoid going out by car. You get all the week-end drivers whizzing round like mad things, looking for a pretty place to park and leave behind all their rubbish. We've even had some impertinent enough to sail up to the house, and ask if we did teas!" Her expression was one of such outraged dignity that Beth could hardly keep her face straight. As they walked slowly out of the car park towards the shops, she said: "What happened?"

Mrs. Thornburn had a slight twinkle in her eyes. "They were quite rude to poor Mrs. Macdonald, implying that those with big houses like ours shouldn't be so selfish as to hog them to ourselves! I'm no snob, my dear, as I'm sure you know, but I do think good manners are important in this day and age. Well, the man, a big, loud-mouthed character in a flashy car – you know the kind – didn't show any signs of wanting to leave, so I went for David, who was busy writing as usual." She gave a low, reminiscent chuckle. "Ah, that was something to see! He sent him packing, after a few well chosen words. He didn't lose his temper, he rarely does, but he can freeze anyone if he chooses."

Yes, Beth thought grimly, I'm sure he can. The more she heard about him, the less was she looking forward to working with him. On their brief encounters he had shown a cool politeness, but there was nothing friendly in his manner. It was in such marked contrast to Mrs. Thornburn, the soul of warmth, or Giles, who had made her feel so at home right away with his outrageous compliments, and sense of fun. Of the two men, David was by far the stronger personality, she sensed. And he knew Alan well! The thought came to her suddenly as they walked along the pavement, and she stopped. Yes,

Alan had gone white when he'd seen him. . . .

"What is it? Seen something you like?" Beth realised Mrs. Thornburn was watching her curiously. Beth
shook her head.

"It was nothing, really. I was just wondering if Mr.
Benedict knew anyone at the office in London."

"Why, yes," she nodded. "Of course he knows both
Hutchinson, and Green, quite well. As a matter of fact,
John Green's sister Cissie – a ridiculous name, short
for Cecilia of course – lives just a few hundred yards
away from cousins of mine, and they're old friends.
In fact, it's through them that Green came into the
business ten years ago."

Beth hardly heard the last words. So that explained
why David Benedict had been walking past the cottage
that Sunday morning. What luck that he should be staying there that fateful weekend! It was foolish to dwell
on it, but her thoughts kept coming unavoidably back
to it, and the expression in his grey eyes. . . .

"I'm sorry. What did you say?"

The old woman was watching her intently. "I thought
we might go in here and have a coffee while we mapped
out our plan of campaign for the shops."

"Yes, of course." Beth pushed open the door and
took Mrs. Thornburn's arm as they threaded their way
through the tables filled with shoppers like themselves.
She greeted several of the older ones as they made for
a table in the corner.

"Ah, that's better. I used to come here with Miss
Withers, your predecessor," she waved a beringed hand
at someone behind Beth. "She left me to get married –

much to my surprise, though of course, I was delighted for her, my dear." She looked up to order coffee and cakes from the plump, middle-aged waitress, and continued: "When I say I was surprised, it was just that she was so much older than you, and a rather prim-faced girl, though very efficient, of course."

"Mrs. Thornburn," Beth said, "did she also do typing for Mr. Benedict?"

For some unknown reason the old woman became flustered. Normally direct in her glance, she looked round as if impatient for the waitress, then reluctantly answered: "Well, yes, for a – er – short time, anyway."

Beth's heart sank. There was something strange going on. She wanted to know what, but could hardly ask without seeming rude. Yet something must have shown on her face, for her employer asked: "Why, what is it, Beth?"

"I – is he d-difficult to work for?" Beth blurted out.

"Oh, Beth, child! Have I given you that impression?" She began to laugh softly, only stopping as the waitress came back with the coffee. When she had gone, Mrs. Thornburn went on: "No, oh, dear me. It's just that – well, David is a little *reluctant* to have a secretary again – you see, he prefers to type his own scripts out in rough form, then send them off to an agency to have fair copies made. He's a bit stubborn, and we've had one or two arguments about it. However, he's decided to give you a fair trial. We discussed it this morning before breakfast. He says I've bullied him into it, imagine! Me bullying him!" Beth smiled a little, as her employer seemed to expect it, but she didn't feel like smiling inside, and it was an effort. She was cold with dismay. Forcing her tone to be light, she said: "But why do you want him to have a secretary? I mean if he's satisfied with the way he does things now?"

"Because men don't always know what's best for them," Mrs. Thornburn answered firmly. "All this messing about, posting things off and waiting for them to come back, and then checking them – he shouldn't have all that worry and bother, he has enough to do otherwise. You'd be able to take all that burden from his shoulders, possibly deal direct with the studios. He works too hard as it is, and I do so worry about him."

And then Beth knew. "Mrs. Thornburn," she said gently, "that's really why you asked me to come and work for you, isn't it?"

The old lady looked at her, and her face was wistful as she nodded.

"So you've guessed." A little secret smile played round her mouth. "You're a very astute young woman, you know that? I like you very much, Beth. If I'd ever had a daughter, I would have wanted her to be like you."

"Thank you," Beth said quietly. "I'll try not to let you down." Mrs. Thornburn meant so well, there was nothing else she could say. And yet there was the strange impression of something left unsaid.

And so, that afternoon, she began to work for David Benedict. He had told his aunt that Beth was to go to his study after lunch. She went up to her room to wash and make up at two o'clock, feeling as nervous as if she were going for an interview for a difficult job. Uppermost in her mind was the desire not to let Mrs. Thornburn down.

At least she knew exactly where she stood. That helped a little, and a strange determination filled her as she stood in front of the mirror, smoothing a few stray wisps of hair back. So he didn't want a secretary? Then she was going to make him change his mind. Beth knew that she could tackle any reasonable job, was sure of her own abilities. The other incident was to be put firmly at the back of her mind, and forgotten. He hadn't recognised her, and that was the end of the matter. And perhaps she would soon be able to forget Alan as well. Perhaps. . . .

She wore a blue courtelle skirt with a plain white 'secretarial' blouse with long sleeves. Faint hollows showed in her cheeks, and her mouth seemed fuller, but it might have been a trick of the light. She seemed altogether delicate-looking, and smiled slowly. Perhaps it would help to disarm the brute! A touch of lipstick, and Beth was ready to go down. She took a deep breath. This was it!

She knocked at the heavy door to his study, and waited, her heart beating fast, hammering the pulse at her throat so that she was sure he would see.

"Come in." Slowly Beth opened the door, her precious notebook and pen clutched tightly in her hand. He stood by the window, and he turned slowly as she went in.

Dressed casually in thin black sweater and grey slacks, his height and powerful build accentuated by them, he dominated the room. In that instant Beth sensed his resentment too, and knew a momentary flutter of fear, quickly banished. He had no right to feel like this, for he didn't know her. And strangely, it helped to calm her. She would show him!

"Good afternoon, Miss Kendrick," he nodded. "Sit down." He indicated a chair by his paper-littered desk. The room was large, tidier than Beth had expected, and furnished only by desk and two chairs, and several metal filing cabinets. He came and sat on the edge of the desk and looked at her. The gaze was a cold clear one, his grey eyes expressionless as he said:

"Right. Let's get a few things straight before we start. First, I've only asked you here this afternoon to please my aunt, who seems to think I need assistance. I don't, but as I am very fond of her, I occasionally do as she asks for the sake of her peace of mind." He looked round the room. "This is where I do all my writing. I can only work alone. The library is next door. You will do all your typing there, and please understand, I do not wish to be disturbed once I've given you your work. If there's anything not clear, it will have to wait. So to save time, I suggest that you read through the scripts I give you before you leave this room, and ask any questions now. Do I make myself clear?"

"Perfectly, sir." Inwardly Beth raged at his arrogance, but hid it. "Then I won't need this?" she held up her notebook.

"Not today. Now, here are two scripts." He leaned sideways and picked up a thick pile of papers, squaring them slightly on the desk before handing them to her.

"Read those now. It shouldn't take you long to skim through."

Beth looked up in disbelief. Surely he was joking! But there was no trace of a smile on his features, and after a moment he stood up, went over to the first filing cabinet, and opened the top drawer.

She took a deep breath. He was testing her, hoping she would show dismay at the amount to be done, then he would be able to tell Mrs. Thornburn that his new secretary wasn't up to it.

Without saying a word Beth put everything down on the desk, moved her chair a little closer to it, picked up several of the sheets, and began to read. She had to bite her lip to stop the exclamation of surprise when she saw what she was reading, for she sensed that he was watching covertly, to note her reaction. So this was what he wrote! Beth had been thinking all sorts of things, but she hadn't expected to see an episode of *The Trouble-makers*. She knew now what Mrs. Thornburn had meant when she had told her she couldn't watch. But it was important to get through the pages as quickly as possible. He had typed it very roughly; there were pencilled insertions and alterations on nearly every page, but his writing was clear, and the typing good enough to spot any glaring or puzzling errors almost immediately. Beth read on silently, not trying to assess the content, merely to see that the words had logical continuity.

The pile at one side diminished, and grew at the other as she read. When she had finished the first script she looked up, to see him standing watching her, a strange expression on his face.

"I've finished that one," Beth said, "and I think I understand everything. Would you like me to begin typing, or finish reading the second?"

"You can type it now," he answered. "Is it easy to follow?"

"Yes, thank you." She stood up and picked up all the papers. "If you'll tell me where the paper and carbons are, I'll begin."

"I'll show you." He went and opened a door, and Beth was surprised to find herself in the library. She turned to him in astonishment. "I didn't notice this door yesterday," she said.

"No?" his tone implied that he wasn't surprised, and she chided herself inwardly for her foolishness. Stupid of her to give him any opportunities to be sarcastic. He didn't like her, that was obvious. She had done nothing to possibly offend him, yet his manner was one of thin politeness, the very minimum acceptable. Beth returned his dislike equally – but didn't intend to let it show, and that would be to her advantage, she knew. He didn't want her, he had taken her on with the greatest reluctance simply to humour his aunt. That in itself was rather surprising, for he had already made an impression as a man who cared little for anyone's feelings. She still remembered the expression on Mrs. Thornburn's face when he had refused dinner on Beth's first evening there.

Alone in the library, the communicating door firmly shut, Beth sat down and tried to get her thoughts in order. She let out a sigh of relief and picked up the rough script. It was incredible to think that a man like

41

David Benedict could write such material.

It was a popular weekly series on commercial television, about two suave modern-day Robin Hoods, who were a mixture of all the heroes from all the series Beth had ever watched – but whose escapades had caught the imagination of an adventure-starved audience, and made them into cult figures. It wasn't rubbish; it had complicated plots and lots of twists, hair-raising chases, fights, and beautiful girls, and surprisingly unpredictable endings. Beth rarely watched it, but Judith did, mainly because she was at the dreamy stage over one of the heroes, Jon Craig, played by an Irish actor of great charm called Sean O'Donnell. Beth smiled to herself, picturing her sister's face when she told her that she was typing out the words her hero would speak. It would raise Judith's prestige no end at school!

Once Beth began to type, all time was lost. She found it tiring, not being used to the different format of scripts, but gradually, as the pile of finished pages mounted, she found it becoming easier, and more, discovered a certain satisfaction in the work.

Beth heard the door open, then David Benedict's voice. "You'd better finish now, Miss Kendrick. It's nearly five, and I don't want my aunt to accuse me of overworking you."

She looked up to see him standing in the doorway, the light behind him silhouetting him darkly, as it had in the garage. Quickly she stood up, obscurely frightened of him. "I'll leave everything on the desk," she said, wanting suddenly to get away. "I'll begin again in the

42

morning, unless Mrs. Thornburn wants me for any letters."

He smiled and walked slowly towards her. "I don't
think she will, do you? How are you managing?"

"Very well, thank you." Beth watched him pick up
the top sheet of her work and glance at it in the light
from the desk lamp. He frowned, and looked at her. "I
thought you'd done scripts before?"

Beth's heart gave an unpleasant lurch. "I h-have, but
only –" she began, caught off balance by the scorn in
his voice.

"Then surely you know that the characters' names,
and the directions, are always typed in red?"

Beth stared at him dismayed, feeling a flush creep up
from her neck. So much for efficiency! Nobody had
said anything about that when she had typed out Judith's
school play last year. Her voice was barely a whisper as
she answered, "I'm sorry, I didn't know."

"You didn't know?" His voice was a whiplash of
contempt. "My aunt assured me you were an expert on
scripts."

Beth was silent. There was nothing she could say to
that. She swallowed hard, hating him. "I'll do them
again in the morning," she said quietly. Her hands trembled with the urge to hit that mocking face.

"You needn't do that. Carry on with this one as you
are doing, and underline what's necessary in red when
you've finished. I'll find you a red pen in the morning. Apart from that, you seem to have been working
very quickly."

"I'll do the next one properly, don't worry. May I go now?"

He nodded, and Beth could barely see the expression on his face, for only the desk light cast a soft golden glow on the papers. The rest of the room was shadowed. There was silence in the room, and a sudden wash of fear swept over her. Her heart beat faster, and she had the urge to escape this hard, ruthless, attractive man. Beth sensed that he could read her thoughts, and like some stupid child she moved away and switched off the light. Now only the path of gold from his study lit her way to the door.

"Just a moment." His hand came on her arm, and she flinched and jerked away at the tingling shock of his touch. His laugh sounded harsh. "Don't jump like a frightened rabbit," he said softly. "I was only going to stop you falling over that stool." He bent and picked it up, then strode to the switch by the hall door, flooding the room with light. Beth walked past him, out of the room, and went upstairs. There, in her bedroom, she was swept by a wave of loneliness and homesickness. It was all turning out different from what she had imagined, so very different.

Mrs. Thornburn and Beth ate together that evening. She felt a little better, seeing the old lady's cheerful face. She so wanted Beth to enjoy working for David that she had to pretend everything was well, and that she had found the work interesting, which at least, in a way, was true.

"A programme of his is on tonight," Mrs. Thornburn said as they drank coffee. "Would you like to watch it?"

"*The Troublemakers*?" Beth was surprised.

Mrs. Thornburn shook her head. "Tch, no, not that one. I certainly can't watch *that*. All those long American cars, and mini-skirted girls! Though I don't tell him," she added, with a little conspiratorial smile. "I wouldn't hurt his feelings for the world!"

And that, Beth reflected wryly, would be quite impossible. She went on: "I mean the other one, *Happy Families*. Didn't he tell you?"

Bemused, Beth shook her head. "I've only looked at one yet."

"Dearie me! He has another one too, *Joe's World*."

"Are there any more?" Beth asked faintly. It was incredible. If she hadn't known her employer better, she would have thought she was joking.

"No, that's all. He has a certain gift, a facility one might say, for writing. It is a legacy, I suppose, from the black sheep of the family, my grandfather's brother, Uncle Rufus Benedict. He wrote 'penny dreadfuls' under the pen name of Jasper Mutch, and was, I believe, a great success – though of course we weren't allowed to talk about him, or even mention his name, when we were children." She leaned back, a reminiscent smile on her face. "Ah yes, those were the days. You know, I might have a picture of him somewhere, taken before he disgraced the family, of course – and he looked remarkably like David too." She shot Beth a shrewd glance. "What do you think, now that you're working for him, eh?"

The question caught her off balance. "I don't know," she admitted. "I think the work will be interesting, and there'll be plenty of it."

Mrs. Thornburn. "Hmm, not committing yourself. Well, don't let him bully you. He writes at terrific speed, at all sorts of hours. Quite frankly, I don't know how he keeps it up, but people like him have a tendency to expect everyone else to be a human dynamo, too. And I didn't bring you here to get yourself exhausted, y'know."

"He was most concerned that you shouldn't think he was overworking me."

"Hmm, maybe. Well, we'll see how you go on after a few days. And just remember, my dear, your weekends are your own. Will you be going home this Friday?"

"I'd like to," Beth answered. "But after this, once a fortnight will be enough. I'm going to save as much as I can from my salary."

"Very wise," the old lady nodded slowly. "I must ask David if he's going down by car. He often does, for he has a lot of friends, and television contacts there, you know – that'll save your train fare."

"Please don't bother," Beth said desperately. The thought of a four or five-hour journey with him was too awful to contemplate.

"Nonsense! Gracious me, he won't mind at all, I'm sure." It was useless to argue. Mrs. Thornburn had made up her mind, and all Beth could do was hope that David Benedict had decided to spend a quiet weekend at home.

She watched the programme, *Happy Families*, with

a sense of unreality. She had seen it so many times before, always enjoyed it, but had never noticed the writer's name. Now it positively leapt out from the screen: 'By David Benedict.' It was so different from *The Troublemakers*, a quieter, easily flowing story about the life and work of two country doctors and their families.

When the first commercial break came, Beth asked Mrs. Thornburn if he ever watched his own shows, and she laughed. "Dear me, no! He says they never do them quite as he would like, so he prefers not to."

"I just don't see how he can find the ideas, or the time, to do them all," Beth said.

"Well, they do have other writers, you know. He only does about one in five episodes of *Joe's World*, for instance, and perhaps one in three of the other, but this one – and I enjoy it – is practically all his."

The evening passed quietly, and Beth went to bed soon after ten. Going to her bedroom window, she opened it, and looked down. The light was on, and faintly across the dark night air, came the sound of his typewriter. She wondered when, if ever, he slept.

CHAPTER THREE

Beth was busy typing, a couple of mornings later, when the door from the hall opened and a voice said:

"Good morning, Beth – if I may be so bold as to call you that."

She turned to greet Giles, standing by the door.

"Good morning, Mr. Benedict."

"Mr. Benedict!" He walked across towards her, shaking his head. "That's enough of the formality. Giles, if you please."

He was dressed in a sports jacket, warm white sweater and cavalry twill trousers, and looked extremely smart. He sat on the edge of her desk, and looked at her, then jerked his head towards the connecting door. "Is my dear coz there?" he asked in a stage whisper.

"Yes. Writing. I don't think he likes being disturbed."

He laughed. "That I already know. Wouldn't dream of it. Of course, all writers are a bit, you know –" he tapped his forehead significantly, "– but cousin David takes the biscuit. Quite mad, I assure you. Apart from *that*, though, he's not bad, as cousins go."

He had cheered Beth immensely by coming in. The contrast between the two men was enormous. If only she could feel relaxed, and enjoy talking, to her new employer as she did with his cousin, everything would be so much easier. As it was, David Benedict made her feel all fingers and thumbs, a condition she tried to cover by adopting a pose of cool politeness and calm.

Whether it fooled him or not, Beth didn't know, but he continued to treat her as if he was reluctant to have her there. The awful thing was that she couldn't tell anyone about it. She was the stranger in the camp, the alien. Even Mrs. Thornburn, whom Beth liked and respected tremendously, would think she was silly. There was nothing tangible about his hostility, just an intolerable tension whenever they were alone. She had to try and dispel it, but it would take time, and meanwhile she was on her own. She had made a bad start, not knowing about the red for the scripts. Beth didn't intend to make any more mistakes, if she could help it. And talking to Giles could be a mistake. If her new 'boss' came in, he would assume the worst, Beth was sure. Quietly, she said: "I hope you don't mind if I get on, only –" she hesitated, and looked to the connecting door.

"Phew! He's certainly got you trained. Don't, I beg you, my dear Beth, don't let him turn you into a nervous wreck like the late lamented Miss Thing."

"Miss Withers, you mean?"

He clicked his fingers. "That's the name. Poor girl," he shook his head sadly.

"B-but I thought she left to get married?" Beth stammered.

He lifted a cynical eyebrow. "Aha, so *that's* what he told you, is it? Don't you believe it. *That's* the official version." He lowered his voice. "She vanished. Just like that – pouf! Gone."

Beth's blood froze – and then she saw the faintest suspicion of a grin on his wide mouth, and said: "How could you! I believed –"

"Ssh! Don't shout. You'll have him in. Anyway, I kid you not. He'll be a real tartar to work for. Personally I'll give it three weeks before you throw his typewriter at him and tell him what to do with his scripts."

"No," Beth shook her head. "You're wrong. Thanks for the friendly advice, even if you did scare me half out of my wits. I shall think of you whenever I feel like gnashing my teeth, and perhaps I'll laugh instead." She picked up a clean sheet of typing paper and rolled it into the machine. Giles leant over and picked up the page she had just finished, his hand resting lightly on her shoulder. And at that moment, David Benedict walked in.

He nodded to Giles. "Morning, Giles," and his grey eyes rested on Beth briefly, and for a second there was a spark in them of something she couldn't fathom, something that made her uneasy. What was he thinking?

She bent her head to the typewriter, and Giles stood up and moved away, casually.

"Morning, cousin. Can I have a word with you about old Larrimer?"

"You'd better come in the study." With the briefest look at Beth, he put a bundle of typescript on the desk and said: "You might as well put that away in a drawer. You can do it when you're ready."

The two men went out, and she began another page of the adventures of Jon Craig and his partner, Brett Wilde.

Friday morning, Beth took Mrs. Thornburn to the village of Appledore in the Rover. She was visiting a friend who lived in a cottage there, and she told Beth to call back for her in an hour or so. As she was pretty sure she would get lost if she ventured far, Beth decided to go back to the house, and prepare her things for the journey to London. She wasn't looking forward to it, for she was going with David Benedict in his car.

Beth slowed down for the narrow turn into the drive. As she did so, she saw a flash of blue in front of the car, and braked, swerving slightly, and nearly hitting one of the high stone posts that guarded the entrance. Even as she got out, to see what she had so nearly hit, a child stepped out from a rhododendron bush, a girl of about seven, wearing a light blue anorak over grubby trousers which were tucked into wellingtons.

"What are you doing?" Beth demanded. "Do you know you nearly got run over?" Shock made her voice harsh, and the child looked up blinking, red-cheeked, like a rosy apple, her hair short and dark, like a boy's.

"I saw you," she answered. "It's all right, I saw you." She might have been reassuring Beth, so earnest was her manner, and the girl relaxed slightly, smiling.

"Do you live here?" Beth asked. For all she knew, it could be a child of one of the gardeners. Two brothers, George and Arthur, lived in adjoining bungalows on the estate, and their wives did all the cleaning at Benedict House.

The child shook her head. "There?" this with a contemptuous lift of her thumb towards the house. "Not me! I live in't village."

"But that's a few miles away. Won't your mother be wondering where you are?"

She looked at Beth as if she were slightly mad. "Me mum? She don't mind. She's got the young 'uns to bother about – and anyway she thinks I'm at school."

"Oh, you're playing truant." Beth looked down at her with a mixture of dismay, and fellow feeling. The temptations to skip school for a day must be great, with miles of country to explore, but on the other hand, she was so young to be wandering about alone, and Beth felt a kind of responsibility for her. She held out her hand. "Come on," she told the child, "I'll take you home."

A frown appeared. "Ay, no, me mum'll wallop me."

"But I can't leave you here – it's going to pour down," Beth said, with sudden inspiration. And indeed the sky had gone dark, with low clouds chasing each other quickly across it.

The child looked up, then at Beth, resignedly. "Well, okay," she shrugged. "I might as well. I was a bit fed up anyway. I can play with our Tony – he's too young for school yet, but he's more fun than that baby of ours, he cries all the time, makes me sick." Still talking, she got into the car, and Beth turned it round and drove off back the way she had just come.

She left the child at the door to her cottage, and decided to spend the remaining half hour walking round the village, as the helpful clouds had miraculously swept over and gone.

Beth told Mrs. Thornburn about the incident as they drove back, and she shook her head. "That'll be Christine Newton. She's a real little tomboy, always running off from home or school. You did right to take her home, my dear, it was very kind of you. I don't suppose you watched her actually going in the house, did you?"

"Well, no," Beth admitted. "But I thought –"

"Hmm, she probably waited till you were out of sight, and scampered off again."

Beth sighed. So much for her good deed, and a wasted half hour!

"Never mind," Mrs. Thornburn must have heard the sigh, for she patted Beth's arm reassuringly. "She always finds her way home. If you see her again up at the house, tell me. I'll have a word with her."

And the subject was left at that.

Beth was busy the rest of the day, until four o'clock, when David Benedict came into the library as she typed away. Nearly at the end of a page, she was conscious of him standing by the door, but she finished it before she looked up, unrolling the paper and separating the carbons as she said: "Did you want something, Mr. Benedict?"

"Yes. Finish now. Can you be ready in half an hour?"

She stood up, straightening the papers. "Yes, of course. And thank you for offering me a lift to London. It's very kind of you."

He inclined his head slightly, a dry smile at his mouth. "A pleasure, Miss Kendrick."

And with that he went back into his den. Beth pressed her lips together tightly. He looked as if it was anything but a pleasure, and she would certainly have preferred to go by train. Her one slight consolation was that she was saving the fare.

Exactly half an hour later she was standing on the front steps, taking her leave of Mrs. Thornburn, while

David went for the car.

She regarded Beth curiously, head tilted slightly to one side as she asked her: "Well now, Beth, your first week is over. And do you think you'll like your new job?"

"Of course. And thank you for everything." But inside, Beth wondered. Impulsively she bent and kissed the old lady's wrinkled cheek, and was startled to see her eyes fill with tears. "Oh, Mrs. Thornburn, I'm sorry," she faltered, as she heard the car roaring up from the garage.

The old lady blinked her eyes rapidly. "Sorry? For what? That was the nicest thing you could have done. Off you go, and have a safe journey." She turned to David, who had come up the steps. "Don't drive too fast, dear, you know how I worry."

"I won't, so stop fretting," he bent to kiss her cheek, and it struck Beth again, this contrast in his behaviour to his aunt and to herself. Still, it was none of her business, and at least he didn't make his aunt feel unwanted. He seemed to have a genuine affection for her. They went down the steps, and his fingers touched Beth's briefly as he took the weekend case from her. "Get in. I'll put this on the back seat," he said.

A minute later, they were off in the super new maroon XJ 6. Beth hadn't known what they would be going in, never having seen his car. Since Monday he had not been out in it. She looked at him covertly as they slowed down for the gates, and on an impulse, to dispel the rather tight atmosphere that existed, said: "I nearly had an accident here this morning. A little girl ran across

54

in front of the car, just inside the gate." She saw him frown, then he looked at the road before driving swiftly out.

"I imagine it was that little menace from the village, Christine Newton."

"Yes, it was. Your aunt told me about her. Does she often come this way, then?"

Changing gear, he accelerated, and the powerful car leapt smoothly forward, almost taking her breath away. There was silence for a few moments, then he answered: "She haunts the grounds. It's a wonder you haven't seen her before now."

"That was the first time. When I asked her if she lived at Benedict House – I thought she might be one of the gardener's children – she sounded as if the idea was –" Beth stopped, realising that it wouldn't be very tactful to repeat her words, and then heard him laugh.

"She sounded as if the idea was appalling? It's all right, you don't need to spare my feelings, Miss Kendrick."

So infuriating was the cynicism in his tone that she had to bite back the retort that came to her lips. Instead she looked out of the windows at the roadside, hedges and stone walls, and hills receding greyly in the background. She decided not to speak again, unless he spoke first. And so for the next half hour they drove in silence. Then he put the radio on, and she listened indifferently to a mish-mash of pop, interspersed with frenetic chat from a D.J. At least, she reflected wryly, it was better than listening to him.

It grew darker outside as they drove swiftly along

the motorway. Nothing overtook them and they sped smoothly past all the other vehicles as if they were crawling. It was with surprise that Beth saw the needle on the speedometer hovering round eighty. Alan had always driven fast, and she had never liked it. Yet now she was perfectly calm. David Benedict was a good and skilful driver, the car was warm and comfortable. She sat back against the well padded seat, and thought about her new life. What a lot she had to tell Mum, and Judith. . . .

"We're here, Miss Kendrick." Beth's arm was being shaken, not ungently, and she opened her eyes. What on earth was going on?

"Take it easy," a lazy voice came from beside her, and she turned to see David Benedict sitting beside her, a look of amusement on his face, one arm resting lightly on the steering wheel as he watched her face. She looked outside the car. They were parked in a street that was very familiar.

"Have I been asleep?" Beth asked foolishly.

"For about two hours, yes. And now we're near your home – I think, and as I'm now slightly lost, I had to wake you."

"But –" she was almost too stunned to speak, "I thought you'd drop me off at a tube station. I only live a few roads away." She felt confused. Why had he done this? Surely he should have been only too glad to get rid of her? And yet, judging by where they were, he must have gone considerably out of his way.

He switched on the engine. "Which way?" he said abruptly.

"First left, then third on the right. I live half way down the road. It's very kind of you to bring me this far. I didn't expect –"

"I always do the unexpected," he answered quietly, and they drove on. A few minutes later they were outside Beth's small semi-detached home.

"Thank you," she turned to him. "Would you like to come in for a cup of coffee?"

He shook his head. "No, thanks. I'm meeting someone at ten." He reached over to the back seat, and handed Beth her bag.

"I'll see you on Monday morning," she said. "Goodbye, Mr. Benedict, and thank you again for the ride. It was very kind of you."

"I'm going back to Derbyshire Sunday tea-time." He leaned forward to open her door, and for a moment their bodies touched. Beth smelt the faint, woody tang of after-shave, then he moved back, and she was out of the car. As she bent to shut the door, he added: "Be ready for five o'clock Sunday. Goodbye, Miss Kendrick." She was left standing on the pavement, watching his tail lights vanish down the road. He had not given her the chance to reply, to say no. She shivered slightly in the cold air, and for a moment the question teased her, did she want to refuse?

They talked until past midnight. Both her mother and Judith were equally fascinated by the fact that David Benedict wrote for television. But they wanted details of the house and grounds as well. Beth told them about Mrs. Macdonald and Anne, and George and Arthur and their wives, and of the orders delivered from the best shops in Buxton, the laundry, Mrs. Thornburn's own hairdresser who came once a week to do her beautiful grey hair, everything she could remember, until her mind reeled with the effort.

Judith yawned sleepily and tucked her legs more firmly under her.

"Oh," she wailed. "Just think – *two* whole days before I can tell the girls! I'll burst before Monday, honestly." She sighed deeply. "And didn't he say anything about Jon Craig – I mean Sean O'Donnell?"

Beth shook her head firmly, catching the quick smile from their mother. "Nary a word. In fact he doesn't even watch the programme."

"Funny man!" Judith opened her eyes wide in disbelief. "What's *he* like, anyway? Is he gorgeous and dreamy, or short and fat?"

"Yes, go on, dear," her mother added. "What is David Benedict like? You let him bring you all the way home, and never even asked him in – what must he have thought?" She shook her head.

"I did ask him in, but he was in a hurry to get somewhere. And he's – well –" Beth stopped, lost for words. How could she describe him? Every inch of his face was imprinted on her mind, yet she couldn't put it into words. Suddenly, she didn't want to. She shrugged and said casually: "Oh, well, he's tall, dark-haired. Quite good-looking in a ruthless sort of way, I suppose –"

"Ruthless," sighed Judith. "Mmm, delicious," she closed her eyes. "I can just see him – has he fallen for you?"

58

Beth burst out laughing. "Him? No! He's barely civil to me. I don't think he's interested in women – or anything except writing. He spends all his time in his study, doesn't even eat with us, and most nights he's typing away into the small hours."

"And why's he come to London?" Judith leaned forward, eyes shining. "I bet he's got a beautiful mistress tucked away in a flat –"

"Judith, really!" their mother interrupted, a look of shocked amusement on her face. Beth let them argue the point, in her mind's eye seeing him again, just before he had dropped her off. He could be going to a woman. She had told them she didn't think that he was interested in them, but in her heart Beth didn't believe it to be true. There was an aura of tremendous virility about the man, a sexual appeal – and Beth knew something suddenly that she had been trying to ignore all the week. She too was coming under the spell of that magnetism. If she wasn't careful, she might find herself falling for him. And that would never do, for it was bad enough working for him as it was.

Beth had run away from one bruised heart, she had to see that it didn't happen again. For if Alan's world and hers were incompatible, how much more was this one. David Benedict had been born to wealth, he walked and talked with all the authority that only years of breeding, and money, can bring. And he didn't like her. She had been forced upon him, and he, not unnaturally, resented it, even though he was coming to find her work satisfactory. But there was something more, something she didn't understand. It was as if he wanted to hurt her. She had done nothing to him. Occasionally, during the week, she had wondered if he remembered her from the cottage, but even if he had, what of it? It was none of his business, and even if he thought the worst about the visit, he would hardly let it affect a working relationship. No, Beth decided, she would never know why he had taken such a dislike to her. She would just have to accept it. Yet it made it so much more difficult to understand why he had brought her all the way home, when he didn't have to.

The two days passed all too quickly. At quarter to five on Sunday, Beth was ready, determined not to keep him waiting a second longer than necessary. When he rang, she would go straight out. She was in the bathroom at ten to five when the bell rang, and when she ran downstairs, it was to hear voices from the living room. She hesitated a moment outside the door, praying that Judith wasn't asking him questions about Jon Craig. Oh, if only he hadn't come early! She pushed open the door and went in. Her mother, Beth noticed in one quick glance, was looking quite flushed and pretty. She was sitting on the settee, smoothing her hair back with fluttering fingers as she looked up at him standing on the fireside rug, jingling his car keys. Judith stood behind her mother, for once tongue-tied. The instant impression Beth had was of overwhelming charm. For some unknown reason, David Benedict had set himself out to captivate her mother and sister – and was succeeding. Both were mesmerised. Neither saw her; she might not have been there. It was David himself who broke the spell. He stopped in mid-sentence and looked at Beth.

"Hello," he said.

Her mother came back to earth, and stood up. "There you are, love. Mr. Benedict was just telling us about some trouble he had on the way here. Fancy, a demonstration – and in this weather too! Are you sure you won't have a coffee before you go?"

He looked at his watch, his expression regretful. "I'd love to, Mrs. Kendrick, but I think we'd better set off now." He turned to Beth. "If you're ready?"

"Yes." She hugged her mother, and then Judith. " 'Bye, darlings. I'll try and come in a fortnight."

"Will you?" Judith's eyes shone as she turned to David. "Will you be bringing her if she does?" Beth could cheerfully have strangled her!

He smiled. "I really don't know. Why?"

Judith bit her lip as if shocked at her own temerity. "Because if you do, would you – could you *please* try and get Sean O'Donnell's photo for me?" She burst the words out in a rush.

"Oh, I see. I'll try." He laughed, deeply, with amusement, a sound perfectly in keeping with the rest of him, and Beth's mother glanced at her and nodded. Beth knew that look. She found him fascinating. Yes, Beth thought wryly, you would. Anybody would, the way he had been behaving just now. But she didn't have to work for him. Then she would see the other side, one that puzzled Beth more than ever.

The journey back to Derbyshire was a little pleasanter. Beth assumed that he had spent a good weekend, and was feeling sufficiently good-humoured to forget to be sarcastic.

When they were nearly there, she said: "I hope you won't take any notice of Judith. She's only young, and they get these crushes on television stars."

He nodded. "I don't mind. I'll be dictating a few letters tomorrow. Remind me to send one to the studios, and I'll get them to send a photo direct to your sister."

"Thank you. It's very kind of you."

"Is it? I occasionally do these things – makes me feel more human."

For once Beth wasn't annoyed. Perhaps, she thought, she was becoming immune to him. She watched him driving, the long capable fingers firmly on the wheel, grey eyes ahead, his back straight, his profile strong and handsome. And she wondered again that a man such as he should have chosen the life he had, the lonely life of a writer, more, one who turned out the sort of things his own fond aunt couldn't watch, nor he himself.

A strange car was parked at the front of the house as they drove up.

"Hell and damnation." Although the words were said in an undertone, very low, Beth heard them perfectly, and turned a startled face towards him.

He stopped behind the large Mercedes, and looked at her. "Did I offend your sensibilities? If so, I apologise."

Beth felt herself flush as the cynicism in his words. "You surprised me, that's all," she answered. "I wasn't sure if I'd heard right."

"You did. Hop out, Miss Kendrick. I'll put the car away. The Mercedes belongs to my Aunt Rose, Giles' mother." So saying, he pushed the door open, gave Beth her bag, and she watched him go with very mixed feelings. Surely his Aunt Rose hadn't brought forth such a comment? With some trepidation, Beth went in.

The woman who sat with Mrs. Thornburn wasn't a bit like Giles. She turned her head round as Beth went in and she heard Mrs. Thornburn say: "Here she is, Rose. My new secretary, Miss Kendrick. Beth, my sister-in-law, Mrs. Benedict."

Cold blue eyes raked Beth up and down as the blonde, immaculately dressed woman took her hand briefly and limply.

"How d'you do?" She spoke coolly, and made Beth feel as if she had made a *faux pas* in shaking hands. She turned again to the older woman, her high-bridged nose quivering faintly, as if at a bad smell. Her mouth was small, but even though she barely moved her lips when she spoke, her voice had a clear, carrying quality.

"Better than the last one, Lavinia. I never could understand why you had such a plain, horsey-faced gel working for you." Beth tightened her lips. This woman was talking about her as if she wasn't there. Mrs. Thornburn said quickly: "Ring the bell, Beth. We'll have coffee, I think."

Beth did so, then sat down, at her employer's indication, beside her on the settee. Rose Benedict looked at her, then opened her bag and took out a gold cigarette case. She didn't offer either of them one, but lit her own cigarette, then fixed Beth with a cold look.

"Would you be so kind as to bring me an ashtray, Miss – er?"

"Certainly." Beth went and brought one back from the other end of the large room, and put it on a small needlepoint table beside her.

"Thank you." She smiled, but it didn't quite reach her eyes. Anne Macdonald came in, and was asked to bring coffee. Even before she closed the door on her way out, Mrs. Benedict's voice rang out:

"Good heavens, is *she* still here?"

"You mean Anne? Why, yes. Were you expecting her to leave?" Mrs. Thornburn's tone was mild, but Beth sensed her annoyance.

"I thought she'd have got herself married to some local farmer's boy by now," Rose Benedict replied, unabashed. "After all, she is nearly twenty, and what else is there for her?"

"Perhaps she prefers to wait until she meets the right man," Mrs. Thornburn replied quietly. Then, as Anne came in again with a tray: "Thank you, dear. Put it down there, Miss Kendrick will pour."

"Yes, madame." Anne spoke and moved, quietly. She was tall, like her mother, but not shy. Instead it seemed as if she had an air of self-containment, an inner confidence that would not be shaken. Beth saw her glance at Mrs. Benedict as she went out, just briefly, but she noted the flash of dislike. Beth didn't wonder at it.

Even as the door shut after her, Mrs. Benedict said, quite loudly: "Well, Giles seems to have found himself a girl-friend at last."

"Really?" queried Mrs. Thornburn. "Do we know her?"

"Possibly. Colonel Brandrick's daughter Kate. A nice girl, rather quiet. He tells me he's going to a party there next week. Let us hope he'll settle down at last." She had freckles on the bridge of her nose. Beth watched them in fascination as Mrs. Benedict spoke in her high, fluted voice. She would look quite attractive if only she hadn't such a petulant expression. It was clear that Giles took after his father. Beth didn't like the woman, and the sooner she could leave, the better. She had brought several paperbacks with her, and wanted to start one. She wondered where David was, and knew now exactly why he had sworn as he had. With his aunt like that, Beth would keep out of the way, too.

When she eventually made her excuses and left, Beth heard the rhythmic tap of the typewriter from the study, and smiled to herself. David Benedict possessed a cast-iron excuse for getting out of the way!

She went up to bed tired, and only managed two pages of a book before she fell asleep.

Something happened a few days later that in a subtle way changed Beth's life at Benedict House.

It was in the afternoon. Anne brought a letter in from Beth's home with the cup of tea. She opened it, and another, folded envelope fell to the floor. She picked it up, her heart beating faster as she saw Alan's familiar writing. With trepidation, she read the brief covering note from her mother, and then sat there, the tea growing cold beside her as she looked at the envelope with its elegant scrawl. So he was back, and he knew Beth had run away. What would he say?

She suddenly found, to her horror, that she didn't want to know. Biting her lip, she slit the envelope with a paper knife, and began to read. It was brief, and in Alan's way, quite to the point.

"Beth dear," he wrote, and she could almost see him sitting at his table, biting his pen as he searched for words. "I got home two days ago and was told by my dear papa·that you'd upped and left the firm. I was so stunned that I couldn't think straight. If you left because of that silly misunderstanding at the cottage, then I must beg your forgiveness, but I can't in all honesty believe you'd do that. There must be some other reason. So okay, I'm not perfect. Who is? But I'm hurt that you could have left without a word. Could we meet and have a drink some evening? Please write, or phone me, any time. Yours, as ever, Alan."

That was it. Beth looked up, unseeing, her heart cold within her. If ever she had wondered about the rightness of what she had done, she didn't any more. Seeing his words, reading between the lines, was an experience. He had never really cared, at all. She was just the one that got away, and his pride, not his heart, had been wounded.

Beth pushed the letter in her bag. She must answer it, and soon . . .

She shivered, and put a new sheet of paper in the typewriter. Better do it now, while his words were fresh in her mind. Hesitantly at first, she began her answer, then quicker, as the words tumbled out. It was easy, so

66

much easier than she'd thought to tell him that the weekend at the cottage had been a minor incident – but one that had made her realise just how far apart were their worlds.

Beth found herself phrasing it kindly, almost as if she didn't wish to hurt him, as indeed she didn't. To her surprise, all bitterness was gone. She had only a kind of pity for him, and there was no trace of the love she thought she had once cherished for him. As she finished the second page, she heard the faint sound of the door handle turning, and panic-stricken, pushed the two sheets in the middle of the script she was typing.

It wasn't until night time that Beth remembered, and she sat bolt upright in bed, a cold wave of dismay sweeping over her as she realised what she had done. How could she have forgotten the letter? Yet she had, and it was still downstairs in the office, and at any minute it was possible for David to go and take the sheets of script, to check through them. What she had written was intensely personal, for no one except Alan to read.

Beth scrambled out of bed and pulled on her blue nylon housecoat and slippers. And as she crept down the silent stairs she prayed that he would be too busy to hear her. She held tightly to the banister as the mellow notes of the grandfather clock in the hall boomed twelve. It provided a welcome cover as she ran across the hard tiled hall floor, and opened the library door. All she had to do now was take. . . . Beth stared in disbelief at the desk as she switched the light on. The pages of the script were gone.

"Oh, no!" she must have spoken aloud, for even as

67

she turned back to the door, ready to switch off the light, she heard David's exclamation, and whirled round again to see him standing in the doorway from his study, frowning.

Beth instinctively pulled her housecoat closer about her. "I came down for something –" she began, and stopped as he moved towards the desk.

"A letter?" he gave her a level glance as he bent to open the top drawer.

"Yes," she answered slowly. There was something disturbing in his voice, some note of chilling reproof that came across clearly.

He opened the drawer and carefully lifted out the two sheets of paper. Putting them on the desk as she slowly moved nearer, he said: "I took the script back about an hour ago. I found these," his finger flicked them lightly, almost contemptuously, "– in the middle. So I put them in the drawer, as I imagined you'd be looking for them in the morning." He straightened up slowly, and watched Beth walk the last few feet to the desk. Her heart was beating erratically. There was something that frightened her about him, but she didn't know what it was. Had he read what she'd written to Alan? It would be an almost irresistible temptation to most people, and yet. . . .

"No," he spoke softly, but his words were as hard as tempered steel, and Beth flinched, for it seemed as if he read her thoughts.

"No, I didn't read your letter. I was brought up not to read other people's correspondence, and so far have kept to that precept."

68

"I didn't think –" she began.

"No? Then why sneak down like a thief in the night? It would have waited until morning." Icily he interrupted, and Beth wondered what she had done to so rouse his anger. She was at a distinct disadvantage, dressed as she was, and feeling uncomfortable. So much so, that as she went to take the letter from the desk, her slipper caught in the thick carpet, and she stumbled. Even as she felt herself falling, Beth was caught and held. It was only for a moment, a heart-stopping instant in time, but in that moment something happened. As she breathlessly said: "Thank you," and moved herself free, she saw his face. His eyes were suddenly dark and shadowed, his mouth. . . . Beth wanted, absurdly, to kiss him, and horrified, moved away, utterly confused. Snatching up the letter, she stammered: "I – I'm sorry if I – I disturbed you," and fled.

The memory of that incident stayed with her. Even after she had put the letter away, unable to read it again, she remembered how he had looked, the way he had held her. With any other man, she would have sworn he had been about to kiss her – but it was too absurd for words. That was the last thing David Benedict had in mind.

Beth's whole being was still in turmoil, for she knew something she could no longer deny. She loved David Benedict. It was hopeless, stupid, but heaven help her, she could no longer ignore it. How could she go on working with a man so cold, so hostile? Yet she must. She had run away once. Some time, the running had to stop. And that was now.

69

CHAPTER FOUR

Thus began a new phase in Beth's life at Benedict House. As the days, and then weeks, passed, she grew to accept the situation, even derive some humour from it. Ironic that she should find herself working for a man she had first seen on that disastrous weekend. That it should have been the expression she had seen – or imagined – on his face, that had triggered the final parting with Alan.

She was now working four days a week for him, and one, officially, for Mrs. Thornburn. She went home on alternate weekends. She was saving more money than she had ever been able to before, and everything would have been perfect, except for one thing.

Occasionally David drove her up to London. Judith thought he was wonderful, especially since he had arranged for Sean O'Donnell to write her a short letter with the photograph. It had done wonders for her popularity at school, and she kept saying Beth was an idiot not to see how marvellous David was. Little did she know! Under the calm exterior she presented to the world, Beth's heart cried out for him. She was in love, deeply, for the first time in her life. That was what those few magic moments in the library had done for her. For him, they might have had an entirely opposite effect. His eyes, whenever they met hers, were impersonal and cold. She was in love with a man who was barely aware of her existence, except as a secretary.

It was the week before Christmas. Beth went into the library to begin her morning's work, and as she looked towards the window, the first snowflakes of the winter began to fall. Putting down her bag she went across to the window and looked out. The soft white flakes drifted gently downwards to rest on the gravel path and grass. Starlings walked like little old men across the lawn, looking in vain for worms, and in the distance the trees were grey and pale.

It was so quiet and peaceful, and there was a kind of beauty about it. Any snow that fell in the city was soon churned into brown slush. Yet here it would stay and cover the countryside with a blanket of white. Beth sighed, touched by the beauty of it all, wishing her mother and Judith could come and see it. But they were nearly two hundred miles away, and in a few days she would be going home to them for Christmas. Already London seemed a lifetime away. Benedict House was like a second home, one Beth loved. Yet she should not even think it, she knew. It was not her home, never would be. There was something, a deep-rooted atmosphere of calm and content that was timeless, and which had already soaked into her bones. Mrs. Thornburn was a wonderful person, Beth got on well with Mrs. Macdonald, and fairly well with Anne, who was difficult to know. She wasn't unfriendly, merely withdrawn. Beth felt sure that Giles had a lot to do with it. From little things said – and left unsaid, on his frequent visits, she had begun to think that he and Anne were attracted to each other. And yet he was still his flirtatious self with Beth. He made it difficult for her with David. She did nothing to encourage him in any way, but it was always the same. David would manage to come in at just the wrong moment, and things would seem vastly different from what they actually were.

Giles' mother, Rose Benedict, was a bitch. She resented Beth and thought she was far too well treated for a mere secretary, to use her own words, loudly spoken so that Beth couldn't avoid hearing. She also implied that Beth was keeping well in with Mrs. Thornburn for what she could get out of her. It was all cleverly done, and the older, gentler woman was no match for her acid-tongued sister-in-law. Perhaps that was why David so resented his aunt, although her behaviour changed considerably on the rare occasions that he was with her. She lived with Giles in a beautiful small house about a mile away from Benedict House. Beth had taken Mrs. Thornburn there once, and been stunned at the elegance and beauty within. It was exquisite, a cameo compared to the ponderous elegance of the older, larger house. Yet Rose Benedict, for all the beauty that surrounded her, was not a happy woman. The lines of discontent were deeply etched on her face, and although she idolised Giles, it was an unhealthy, smothering love, the type that seeks to possess.

It was a wonder he stayed so unspoilt by it all. He was always pleasant and charming to everybody, and Beth liked him very much. But that was all. Her heart was already committed to another. . . .

"Good morning."

"Good morning, Mr. Benedict." Startled, brought back abruptly to the present by his voice, Beth turned to see him standing by her desk, the inevitable pile of papers in his hand. She felt a warm tide of colour rush to her face as if her thoughts could be revealed. That was the trouble – she was always thinking about him. It was difficult not to, feeling as she did, and working in close proximity to him for so many hours a day. He looked very attractive, dressed casually in brown sweater and matching trousers. He was slim-hipped, but his chest and shoulders were broad and powerful. Beth had seen him playing tennis one day with Giles, on the outdoor court. He moved with the easy grace of a panther across the grass, his powerful strokes sending the ball spinning across the net at a fantastic speed. Mrs. Thornburn, with whom Beth had been walking, had remarked, "They like to keep fit, those boys. Especially David. He says that writing is so inactive, physically, that he needs the change." She had sighed. "He used to help Giles more with the management of the estates, but since you came he does more writing. He says it's easier now that you can type it out straight away."

It was the first time Mrs. Thornburn ever made a direct remark about her nephew's opinion of her work. Beth seized his opportunity. "Do you think he's got over his first – resentment – at having a secretary, then?" she asked.

The old lady looked at Beth sharply, an odd expression in her eyes. "What makes you think he resented you?" she asked.

Beth bit her lip. "I – he made it quite clear. I thought you knew. He told me he'd only agreed to take me on to please you," she stopped, aware that she was sounding remarkably 'sneaky.' "I'm sorry," she added. "I shouldn't have said anything."

"Of course you should!" Mrs. Thornburn snorted, banging her stick on the ground. "No wonder you looked so unhappy those first few days – and I thought it was my fault, dragging you away from London!"

"Oh, no, it wasn't that at all. I – well, it was just that I couldn't seem to do anything right at first. But now it's different. We've got into a good routine, and I enjoy the work, really I do. Please don't tell him what I said."

Again that odd, appraising look at Beth. "Of course not, my dear. So you enjoy your work? Good. Tell me, what do you think about the scripts? Are they interesting?" And the conversation gradually drifted to more mundane matters as they drifted back to the house. The conversation came back to Beth as she began the day's work after reluctantly coming away from the snow, which was fascinating. David had gone back into his study, and she picked up a pile of manuscript. It really was incredible, the speed at which he worked.

She sat down and began to type.

By lunch time the snow was thick upon the ground, and then it stopped. Mrs. Thornburn looked at Beth, her eyes twinkling, across the dining table. "Well, Beth, you think the snow is pretty, no doubt, but it can be a blessed nuisance when it traps us for days."

Beth looked at her in surprise, aware that David, on

one of his rare meals with them, was watching. "You mean, snowed up, literally?"

She nodded. "Why, yes! We can't venture out of doors, which is why we always keep a good stock of tinned and frozen food. Lucky for you it's stopped now, or I might have had to send you packing to London, before it's too late."

Beth looked at her, still unsure whether or not she was joking. Those things happened in the wild of Scotland, she knew, but not in the heart of England, surely! David's low, amused voice broke in.

"I assure you it can happen. I was in Buxton two years ago – only twelve miles away, on my way from Manchester Airport, and I had to stay there in an hotel for two days!" He quirked his lips. "However, it's stopped now, so I shouldn't worry. There's fine weather forecast for over Christmas. I'll run you to the station myself. And now, if you'll excuse me, ladies." He stood up and left the room.

For a few moments there was silence. Then Mrs. Thornton spoke. "My dear, if we've at all worried you. . . ."

"No, of course not," Beth reassured her. "Not at all."

"Because I was going to say you could go now, today, if you wished. I'm sure David will manage."

Beth shook her head. "I wouldn't dream of it. He particularly wants me to finish the latest *Troublemakers* so that I can take it with me and drop it off at the studios."

"Oh, but surely – won't that be out of your way?"

"Well, just a little – but I'm dying to see the place I'm

75

always writing to."

She laughed. "I know. They're fascinating places, T.V. studios. A bit overpowering if you don't know anyone, I should imagine. All those people dashing about looking frightfully worried and busy – and so important! And then you suddenly bump into someone in a lift, or going round a corner, and it turns out to be someone you see every night on the box and they always look so different in the flesh, somehow – smaller!" She smiled. "David took me round once, so that was different, and very nice. He *knew* everyone, you see."

Yes, Beth thought, he would. It was a wonder, with his looks, that they hadn't tried to persuade him to go the other side of the cameras. In a way, she was looking forward to going to a place he must know so well, and to which, indirectly, she owed her job.

Beth should have been warned by the deathly quietness when she awoke the following morning. She found out what had happened when she went to the window and looked out. Everywhere was covered in a thick blanket of white. Even the trees were invisible, with only a thin strip of black trunk occasionally showing, where the snow hadn't caught. It was unbelievable, incredible, but it had happened. It must have been snowing all night.

She washed and dressed, then went downstairs. To her surprise David was sitting in the dining room when she went in. He stood up. "Good morning, Beth."

"Good morning, Mr. Benedict." She went to the sideboard, heart hammering against her ribs. Why should the unexpected sight of him always do this? She caught a glimpse of her face in the mirror above the sideboard as she helped herself to bacon and eggs from the warming plate. He now called her Beth, due to Mrs. Thornburn, horrified at their formality. Yet Beth could never bring herself to call him anything other than 'Mr. Benedict,' and he didn't seem to notice. That was the trouble, he didn't seem to notice anything about her. Yet it wasn't due entirely to indifference, for there were times when she would look round by chance, and surprise a look in his eyes that disturbed her. Almost of dislike, and yet not – it puzzled her. She glanced across at his reflection and at that moment he looked up, and their eyes met through the glass. For a second their glances locked and held, then Beth moved away from the mirror and put her plate on the table. Tension filled the room like an electric current, and to dispel it she said quickly: "It looks as if it's been snowing all night."

"Yes. That's why I'm here now. I'm going to try and get you to the station before it gets any worse."

"But the script. I haven't quite finished –"

"That will have to be left. If you don't go this morning, it'll undoubtedly snow again, and then it could be days before anything gets moving."

And he wanted to be sure she was out of the way before Christmas, Beth thought, as she started eating. On Christmas Eve he and his aunt were visiting Giles' mother.

If she didn't manage to make it home, and Beth suddenly, desperately, wanted to go, then there would be the embarrassment of them having to invite her to Giles' – she knew Mrs. Thornburn wouldn't want her to be at home on her own, even though Mrs. Macdonald and Anne would surely be there.

She stood up suddenly, and pushed her plate away, half empty. He looked up from his coffee. "What's the matter?"

"Nothing. I'll go up and get my things ready."

"Right," he looked levelly at her. "Put your warmest coat on, and gloves. I'll have a spare pair of wellingtons ready."

"Wellingtons?" Beth repeated, her hand on the door. What did he mean?

"We'll be walking to the station," he said drily. "I couldn't even drive the car out of the garage today."

"Then – why – are *you* walking with me?"

"I certainly can't let you struggle through the snow alone, can I? You might get lost." A slight quirk of his mouth seemed to imply that that was very likely.

"It's very good of you," she said hesitantly. Before he could answer, the door was pushed, and Beth moved to one side to let Mrs. Thornburn come in.

"There you are, dear," she greeted Beth. "I imagine David has told you about leaving. But you're to come back if there's any difficulty – the trains might get through, we don't know."

"Couldn't you phone the station?" Beth asked. Her heart was sinking rapidly every minute, and as David came round the table to join them, she could almost feel the impatience emanating from him.

He said: "I tried, but can't get a reply. They're probably not answering – that often happens in this weather."

"Oh." In spite of, or perhaps because of, the horrible sinking feeling inside, Beth persisted: "But if you phone Buxton or Derby – perhaps they'll be able to tell you?"

He smiled grimly. "The main lines will be all right. But Appledore is only on a branch line, an unimportant one that meanders through Derbyshire. They probably wouldn't know, or care. No, there's only one way to find out." He looked at his watch, the impatience scarcely concealed. "I'll go and get my coat and the wellingtons. I suggest you put your shoes in your bag and come down barefoot." And with that, he went out.

Beth turned to Mrs. Thornburn and tried to smile. "I'd much rather go on my own," she told her employer. "It's dragging Mr. Benedict away from work."

"Nonsense," she squeezed Beth's arm. "It will do him good. Besides, I'm not having you trying to find your way alone. David knows a short cut that takes a lot off the road. You'll be there in less than an hour."

Less than an hour! It would seem a lifetime with him. Beth could imagine his face when – if – they arrived at the station. And how much worse it would be if they had to turn back!

"Now off you go and get ready," Mrs. Thornburn nodded brightly, "and don't forget, if you can't make it, you'll have a lovely Christmas here. We'll try and make up for it not being home."

"Oh, Mrs. Thornburn, you're wonderful!" Beth said.

"Nonsense. Away with you, Beth." But she smiled all the same.

Beth thought they wouldn't even get down the drive,

but they did. The snow was four feet deep, soft and powdery, and so difficult to walk through that by the time she saw the tall stone posts she was exhausted, her legs trembling with the effort of pushing through the cold, clinging mass that looked so beautiful and delicate. David looked back. "Keep your fingers crossed," he said. "The road might just be better – if anyone's managed to get through." And with these rather menacing words, he turned and pressed on.

If it was hard for her, it must be twice as bad for him, leading the way, Beth reflected, watching the broad back a few feet in front of her. What was he thinking? She knew he resented having to take her, he had made that quite clear. He was dressed in a dark blue anorak, thick tweed trousers tucked into heavy wellingtons, and he looked a forceful figure pushing a way through the snow, treading firmly, using his hands to sweep soft flurries of it aside as he went. Beth carried his small weekend case; it was the least she could do.

"Right, we'll try the road for a while, then take the short cut, if we can find it." David's voice broke into her thoughts. She immediately agreed. Everything was so quiet that their voices sounded unnaturally loud in the stillness. Nothing moved, except high in the sky, where the birds circled ceaselessly, knowing that there would be no food on the ground for them. Mrs. Thornburn always put bread outside the dining room window each morning, and the regulars waited eagerly. Beth closed her eyes, wishing she could go back and smooth away the snow from a patch of grass, enough to enable the birds to feed. This too was something she shared, with her employer, a pity for all helpless creatures. Beth thinking that he didn't look as if he would ever be sorry for anyone. How different they were, and how true that people are blind to their loved ones' faults. Mrs. Thornburn considered David to be kind and wonderful. Beth knew differently. He was hard, so very hard.

The road was a little easier than the drive had been. Someone had passed by, and a thin, unsteady path had been cut through the snow. They set off a little quicker, David still in front, and went for what seemed like ten miles, but was probably only one, through the anonymous whiteness.

"Right, this way." He suddenly branched away from their little beaten track, and began feeling along the snowy mound that was the wall. "I'm looking for the damned stile. It's buried – ah, yes." He held out an impatient hand, and Beth hurriedly scrambled through the narrow gap. He was doing his best. He had a right to be annoyed with her. He would have been well through a script now, if she hadn't needed an escort. She was nagged by the sudden, guilty feeling that perhaps she should have bought him a Christmas gift. She had asked Mrs. Thornburn, a week or so previously, and she had assured Beth that he hated presents of any kind, although she was sure Mrs. Macdonald and Anne would be pleased at the thought. Beth bought them all presents, and left them wrapped in her bedroom with a note, where Anne would find them when she went up. And now it seemed mean to have left him out. Even if she had only bought him a small bottle of Brut, which would have been highly appropriate. The thought made her giggle as she manoeuvred herself through the narrow incline the other side of the stile.

"All right?" he queried, eyebrow raised in a puzzled way. For a moment they stood quite still, and his hand was under her arm. Beth was overwhelmed by a wave of longing, a desire to have him kiss her.... She pulled her arm away quickly. "Yes, thank you," she said, breathlessly. He looked at her oddly for a moment, his grey eyes resting on her face with a disconcerting expression in them. His glance was always like that, direct and hard, almost as if he read her thoughts. It was absurd, of course. How could he? He was no clairvoyant, and yet the feeling persisted. Before the pinkness in her cheeks betrayed her, Beth turned away, looking round as if wondering where they were.

"Which way now?" she asked, as calmly as possible.

"Just follow me." He struck off in a faintly upward direction, and Beth, not daring to pause, followed him as best she could.

Perhaps they would just go on for ever, struggling through the snow. It certainly felt like it. The cold air pricked her cheeks with its invisible needles, and every breath came out as a cloud of steam that vanished in seconds. Yet it was exhilarating, Beth discovered to her pleasant surprise as she took a deeper breath. Maybe she was getting used to it, but the day took on a different atmosphere at that moment, and as David turned and paused, she felt a fluttering sensation in her stomach. He was higher than Beth, clearly, starkly outlined against the pure white sky, a striking-looking man, and one whom she dreamed about so often and so vividly that she knew every inch of that lean handsome face.

"Give me your case," he said, holding out his arm.

She walked up to him. "It's all right," she answered. "You have enough to do."

"Not now," he pointed ahead of him. They stood at the crest of the rise, and down below in the distance, a cluster of toy houses, vivid against the snow, stood the village, and beyond it the station.

Beth gasped at the sheer beauty of it, so still and perfect, a miniature, remote, somehow untouched.

"But there's nothing moving," she said. "I can't see a soul!"

He grinned. "No. You will when we get nearer. They'll all be busy shovelling snow off their front doorsteps. Come on."

Beth didn't know how it happened. All she remembered was that she started to follow him down the hill, and it was easier going. Something distracted her attention, a bird, moving from a nearby tree, and shaking a profusion of snow as it went, and she moved her head to look at it. Then, as she turned back, she must have put her foot down a rabbit hole. She lurched forward with a cry and pitched straight to the left, towards the steep hillside below. The snow stopped her, but even so she tumbled several yards. Beth heard him shout, and the next second David was running towards where she lay wet and uncomfortable, partly under four feet of snow.

"My God! What happened?" She noticed, absurdly, even above the agonising pain in her left foot, that his face was white.

"I twisted my foot, I think," she managed to say, fighting tears of pain. To have come this far, and for this to happen! But on one thing she was determined. She would not, under any circumstances, cry.

"Up now, carefully." With surprising gentleness he pulled her up, and back on to the rough path. Then he looked down at her, frowning slightly. "How did it happen?"

"I don't know." Beth shook her head helplessly, blinking quickly.

"Are you badly hurt?"

"Only my ankle."

The smothered oath was barely audible. He knelt down. "Which one? I'll have a look."

"The left." She looked down, gritting her teeth so as not to wince as he quickly eased the grey wellington off. He gave a little whistle. "Wow! I'd better get it back on, before the swelling starts."

"Is it – is it awful?" Beth asked faintly.

"Well, you've certainly done something to it. I won't touch it. Come on. We'll get to the village, it's not far."

He helped her along by putting his right arm round her waist, and lifting her left arm to go over his shoulder. Putting her bag in his left hand, they set off.

"Listen," Beth gasped. "If the trains are running, I'll be all right, really. I can get a taxi home from Euston."

Their progress was slow and awkward, as they negotiated the steep snowy path, and he didn't reply for a moment. Then he said: "Don't be silly. It's quite out

84

of the question now.' "

"But –" she began.

"Don't argue," he gave a sigh. "Look, can you imagine Aunt Lavinia's face if I told her you'd sprained your ankle, but got the train okay, and you'll get a taxi from Euston – oh, brother! "

"You don't need to tell her," Beth said, in a quavery voice. It was no use. She was trying to be sensible – and he was making her feel stupid – and somehow unwanted. He intended taking her back to Benedict House, and she would spend Christmas there, and she suddenly didn't want to. His face was set and grim, she saw, as she stole a sideways glance. Oh yes, he disliked her all right. He made that clear in so many countless ways, and she couldn't fight it, because there was nothing tangible to fight, just an atmosphere, a tension barely concealed, and she had too high a regard for his aunt to think of leaving. She had left a place once before, trying to forget a man she had imagined herself in love with. Beth had to learn to grow up, and accept things. Perhaps one day soon she would be able to laugh at herself for her absurd feelings now. She was working for him, that was all it was, the proximity, the irresistible challenge of a man who wasn't interested. . . .

"Does it hurt much?" His voice was almost harsh, like a stranger's.

Beth shook her head silently. She had just put her left foot down, without thinking, only for a second, and the pain had made her gasp. If only he wasn't so near, holding her so closely – and so impersonally. His arms were like bands of steel, and under the shoulder that she clung to, she could feel hard muscle and bone.

"Nearly there," he said, as they came slowly, slowly down, and reached road level. "I'll take you to the doctor's, let him have a look, and then we'll see."

"We'll see." The words had an ominous ring, almost as if he had changed his mind. Perhaps he would let her get the train after all – the pain was so bad that she no longer cared. All Beth wanted to do was sit down and take the weight off it.

One or two people waved to him as they passed the cottages. He was right. Most of them were sweeping up snow from their path, and those that weren't were standing watching the others.

"Here we are." He pushed open a creaky green gate and they went slowly up a snow-free path to a stone bungalow with a wide oak-panelled door. There was a short silence after the sharp buzz of the bell, then an elderly woman opened the door and stood looking crossly at them.

"Surgery's round the back, you know that –" then her face broke into a smile. "Why, Mister David, I didn't see – here, come on in, don't be standing there in the cold."

"Hello, Mrs. Longden, sorry to come in the wrong way, but as you can see, we're in a bit of trouble. This is Beth Kendrick, Aunt Lavinia's secretary."

"How do, miss," the old woman looked her up and down thoughtfully, then hustled them into the kitchen. "Here, sit you down, I'll tell Doctor in a moment. He'll not mind, seeing as it's you. Besides, there's just the regulars at the moment, and they only come in for a gossip." She gave a sniff. "Nothing wrong with them that a good day's work wouldn't cure, eh, me dear?" Again the thoughtful look at her, but with a smile tacked on at the end, to which Beth hastily responded.

Mrs. Longden was cooking lunch. She moved slowly from table to oven, with a pudding basin full of something that looked interesting, then after satisfying herself that the heat was just right, went out.

She was back a few moments later, popping her head round the door like a conspirator. "Come on then, he'll see you now."

With a quick look at Beth, David stood up, and held out his hand.

"Ready?" he said.

CHAPTER FIVE

It was Christmas Eve, and the house was filled with cards, and holly, and a huge decorated tree in the hall. Beth stood at the library window. She had gone in to pick a few books to read that evening, when she would be alone. A wash of homesickness and sadness came over her as she looked out at the silent garden smothered in white. Tomorrow, Sunday, she should have been at home with her own family, enjoying her mother's Christmas dinner, and instead she was here with Mrs. Thornburn and David. She was torn in two, wanting to be in the safe, familiar place on the one hand, yet knowing the sweet agony of watching the man she loved, on the other.

She turned away, wincing a little at the pain from her ankle. It was firmly bandaged, and over it she wore an old slipper. Mrs. Thornburn had lent her a walking stick, and she managed to get around quite well, even though she felt foolish. It seemed a lot of fuss about nothing, yet the doctor, a dour Scot, had told Beth to rest it as much as possible for a week. She had no choice, she reflected, wryly, not with Mrs. Thornburn watching her. She really was a dear, and Beth's accident seemed to have increased her natural tendency to mother her.

It had all been unnecessary too, for the trains weren't running, and most of the main roads for a radius of ten miles were blocked.

Beth heard the faint tap of David's typewriter from the next room; he rarely stopped working. She had never known anyone like him, it was difficult to keep up with the output of scripts from his fertile brain. She knew that in a few days she would be working flat out to type the results. And yet she didn't mind, didn't mind at all. Beth was coming to love his work more than she had ever dreamed possible, and her biggest thrill had been only a few nights previously, when the very first episode of *Happy Families* that she had ever typed had been on television. It was strange, knowing what was going to happen, knowing, even before she saw them, the actions of each character, the expression on his face.

Yet she had a faint tingling of uneasiness about David. He couldn't keep this up indefinitely, this frantic churning out of material day after day non-stop, a ceaseless, endless pile of work. He would burn himself out, make himself ill. Yet who was Beth to tell him? He would laugh at her, or worse, turn on the icy scorn for her interference. She dared not, but she worried just the same, and she had seen the difference in him even in the weeks she had worked at Benedict House; the tiny lines of fatigue round his eyes, the way he would run his fingers through his hair, a grim expression on his face, and the number of cigarettes he now smoked, while working. He wasn't a happy man. Something was driving him on, something Beth could not even guess at. All she could do was keep silent, and help in the only way she knew, by typing efficiently and well, and taking some of the burden from his shoulders.

She picked two romantic thrillers from the shelves and went to join Mrs. Thornburn in the lounge.

Nine o'clock came, and the mellow grandfather clock was striking as Beth walked slowly to the front door with Mrs. Thornburn.

"I do wish you'd change your mind, my dear," she said. "Rose will make you very welcome, I know."

"I'm sure of it," Beth answered. "But I really do feel tired, and my ankle's very sore — besides, I've got a good book, and the television."

She shook her head. "But you'll be alone —"

Beth laughed. "Mrs. Macdonald and Anne are only at George's house, I've got the phone number written down, and it's only a few hundred yards away. And I have Mrs. Benedict's number, by the phone. And thank you for saying I can ring my mother," she added.

"Of course. And don't worry about the time. Be on as long as you like." Her employer patted her hand briskly. "I feel very tempted to stay at home with you, and watch television," she sighed. "But — well, Christmas is traditional, and this is something we do every year."

"I hope you have a lovely time. Be careful on the road."

"We will, and it's not far, only about a mile. Bye-bye, my dear." Mrs. Thornburn kissed Beth and she watched her go down the steps, assisted by David, who had been waiting by the purring car.

Beth stood on the steps and watched them go down the drive, cleared of snow by George and Arthur, with a snow-plough at the front of one of the farm tractors. And the road outside was passable, a wide track having been beaten in it since their vain attempt to reach the station a few days previously.

When they were out of sight, Beth shut the door firmly and walked slowly back into the lounge, where a roaring fire awaited her, and beside it a coffee table with a huge box of chocolates, and her books. It was really very cosy and comfortable, and she settled down after switching on the television.

She tried not to think about David, but her thoughts kept returning, seeing him in that beautiful little house, sitting talking, glass in hand, drinking and laughing, exuding that effortless charm that could so delight and fascinate. Beth had seen it at work on her mother and Judith. And it had worked on Beth, too, even though, with her, he hadn't been trying. She glared at the television. Everyone seemed to be having a marvellous time, waving paper hats and balloons around at an all-star party. Just about everyone. Except her. They would all be there, Giles and his mother, and perhaps local friends. Beth sighed, suddenly quietened by the thought. She wouldn't have enjoyed herself if she had gone, useless to pretend otherwise. They were not her kind, never would be. Giles was friendly enough, there was no trace of snobbery there. Mrs. Thornburn was an absolute darling, there was no other word for it. While David — what of David? Beth watched a margarine commercial with scant attention while the thought of him went through her mind. Easy enough to blame the way he behaved on class-consciousness — yet she knew in her heart that that was not the reason for his cold dislike of her. It was something else, something more. . . . Beth crossed restlessly to the television and turned it to B.B.C. Even there she could not escape from the false jollity oozing out. It was no use. She was in no mood for it. She switched off and began to read.

The house was very quiet. Beth had left all the down-stairs lights on, as instructed by Mrs. Thornburn, but even so, it was with some nervousness that she eventually went up to bed, just after midnight. She was completely alone in a vast house, and didn't know when anybody would be back. She sighed ruefully. It was her own choice, after all. She could have been at Mrs. Benedict's. She shuddered, and walking carefully, using the stick to help her, made her way upstairs.

The bed was warm and comfortable. Beth was almost asleep when she heard voices, and opened her eyes to discover she had left the light on. Slowly she sat up and listened. To her utter surprise she heard Giles' voice saying:

"Come on, love, try and manage the stairs, you'll be all right when you can lie down." A faint moan was the only response, and it made Beth's blood run cold. What had happened? Mrs. Thornburn must be ill. But where was David? Quickly Beth pulled on the only thing to hand, a filmy blue negligee, and went to the door, forgetting her ankle, forgetting all the pain in her anxiety to help her employer. They were coming up the stairs, oh, so slowly. Beth heard them, then, as she turned the corner in the corridor, and saw who it was, she gasped in utter amazement. Giles was helping a very white-faced Anne up the stairs!

"Giles! What's happened? How –?"

He looked up, his normally cheerful face worried. "Beth? Thank God it's you. Can you help Anne into bed? She's feeling ill."

Together they walked slowly back down the corridor, on past Beth's room, to the other end where Anne and her mother had theirs. At the door Beth said to him: "Go and bring a drop of brandy, and – oh yes, a hotwater bottle. If you can't find one, take the one out of my bed, it's still pretty hot. I'll make her comfortable."

Ten minutes later they stood outside her door, which Beth had left ajar. Anne was asleep, her face still pale, but she had been sick, and had assured Beth faintly that she felt much better.

"Thanks, Beth," Giles said. "I'd better tell you, hadn't I?"

She smiled and shook her head. "No, it's none of my business, Giles. The only reason I got up was because I thought you'd brought Mrs. Thornburn back ill."

He laughed. "No. She'll be having a great time at my mother's. It's just – well, Anne and I have been out to-night to some friends. No one knows about us, except her mother – and now you. I love her very much, Beth, and I think – I know – that she loves me. But there are difficulties," he gave a shrug that told much.

They went slowly down the stairs together. In the hall he stopped, and put his hand on her arm. "I'll go now. I guess we both had a little too much to drink, and Anne's not used to it."

"She'll be fine in the morning," Beth assured him. "Though she might have a headache. And Giles, thank you for telling me. I won't say a word, you know that."

As he opened the front door, he turned to her. "I know you won't. In a way it helps to have someone like you knowing about us. Anne – well, she needs someone to talk to. Her mother's not very keen because of the 'difference' as she calls it. I don't give a damn about that – but Anne's so determined not to hurt anyone's feelings – I presume she means my mother's – that she won't listen to reason." He sighed, and Beth saw the strain in his eyes. So many things had suddenly become clear. The looks she had glimpsed between them on Giles' visits, fleeting but puzzling. His mother's dislike of Anne. She almost certainly didn't know anything, but probably sensed an attraction between them, and was determined that it wouldn't come to anything. Poor Giles! With a mother like Rose, Beth could see that he did have problems.

They stood on the steps, the light flooding out from behind them, making the snow glitter like silver. She shivered, and he said:

"Sorry, Beth. You'll freeze out here. I'm a selfish beast, aren't I? Go on in, and back to bed. Thanks for everything, and Beth –?"

"Yes?" she half turned, and he put his head down, and kissed her cheek gently. "Happy Christmas."

"Happy Christmas to you, Giles. Goodnight." She stood and watched him walk off through the snow until he reached his car. He waved to her before getting in, and then drove off.

As she was about to go back in Beth heard a voice say:

"Well, well!" She whirled round to see David step out of the shadows and come towards her. Her heart leapt in sudden alarm in that moment before she recognised him, and she put her hand to her breast.

"You – you frightened me!" she exclaimed. "I didn't know there was anyone there."

"No?" he walked steadily up the steps and followed her into the hall, then shut the front door violently behind him. "No," he repeated, "I'll bet you didn't." There was something about his manner that was disturbing. His eyes met hers, and Beth saw the points of white-hot anger that lit them as he came towards where she stood. He stopped in front of her, towering over her, a powerful figure, immaculately dressed. This wasn't the suave employer, the busy writer, Beth knew, it was a different, somehow frightening man altogether, and in a moment of blinding clarity she knew what he was thinking. Even as he said the words, she knew.

"It's a pity he didn't sneak out the back way," he said. "You did so well – I believed you myself. I felt sorry for you because you were alone. Alone! My God!" he gave a bitter laugh. "And I walked home so that you wouldn't be nervous on your own!" He turned to the door, then slowly back to her, and his well-shaped mouth was twisted and contemptuous. Beth knew exactly what was going through his mind, and a shiver of anger ran up her spine. He had seen something, and without waiting for an explanation, had jumped to the worst possible conclusion. Very slowly and, she hoped, calmly, Beth said: "And what does that mean?"

"Don't give me the wide-eyed innocent look, *Miss* Kendrick. You know precisely what I mean. You've been having a very pleasant time here with my cousin, who assured us, when he left the party hours ago, that he was going to visit an old friend."

"I have not been having a 'pleasant' time with Giles, as you so tactfully put it – and I won't even go into the meaning behind your words, *Mr*. Benedict. As a matter of fact, I spent the evening entirely alone." Beth turned away to go upstairs, aware suddenly of her flimsy attire. Unable to resist a parting shot, because her temper was so thoroughly roused that she was almost trembling, she added: "And even if we had been together – which we weren't – it would have absolutely nothing to do with you."

"Quite right, of course." He spoke loudly, and followed her to the foot of the stairs. "Your lovers should be of no concern to your employer," he added icily.

Beth looked him straight in the eye, temper at boiling point.

"Listen," she said. "I've had enough of this talk. You might be my employer, but I don't have to take disgusting innuendoes like that from you."

"Perhaps you prefer action," he said harshly, and grabbed her. The next second Beth was struggling in his arms as his lips came cruelly down on hers in a searing kiss that went on for ages.

Gasping, she pulled herself free at last and pushed him away.

"How dare you!" she said shakenly. "How *dare* you!"

His eyes blazed back at her. "Quite easily. I don't see why I shouldn't join the queue for your favours. First Alan, now Giles. Who next, I wonder?"

Beth stopped, stunned. "Alan? What do you mean?"

His eyebrows rose cynically. "You've forgotten your weekend at the cottage? You must be a busy girl!"

Raising her arm, Beth slapped him soundly across the face, so hard that it jerked his head to one side. Taking a deep breath to stop herself trembling, she said: "You're revolting and disgusting! I'm going to bed. I'm also going to lock my door, so don't waste your time trying it." And she turned and walked slowly, painfully, upstairs. The pain wasn't entirely from her throbbing ankle. At last she knew the answer to one question. He *had* recognised her. As Beth reached the top of the stairs, she looked back. He stood where she had left him, stroking his cheek. His expression was unfathomable.

It was lunchtime when Beth saw Mrs. Thornburn on Christmas Day. She came home, her cheeks glowing with the cold air, a big smile on her face as Giles helped her up the steps.

"Merry Christmas, my dear," she greeted Beth as she waited by the open door.

"Merry Christmas, Mrs. Thornburn," Beth bent her head to her kiss, and saw Giles signalling, out of the corner of her eye.

It was ten minutes before they could talk, during

which Mrs. Thornburn thought it necessary to explain why she had stayed the night at her sister-in-law's. She had felt too tired for the drive home, but David had insisted on walking home so that Beth wouldn't be nervous. Then she had gone to church in the village, and Giles had run her home. Making the excuse that she had to get some papers, Beth left her sitting comfortably in the lounge enjoying a cup of coffee, and eating chocolates. Giles followed Beth into the library. She listened at the door to David's study, but there was silence. She hadn't seen him, and as far as she knew he was still in bed.

Giles was bursting to ask her about Anne, and as soon as she had come away from the connecting door, he said: "How is she?"

Beth smiled. "Fine. I looked in about eight, when I got up, and she'd just woken. She had a headache, so I gave her two aspirins, and told her mother she wasn't feeling well. I think she's up now, though. Why don't you go to the kitchen and see her? They're preparing lunch."

He shook his head. "No, better not. Just give her a message, will you? Tell her to meet me at the usual place this evening, about nine."

"I will," Beth answered. "Now, we'd better go back or Mrs. Thornburn will wonder what we're up to."

As they went back to the door, Giles said quietly: "You were a brick last night. Thanks, Beth – and thanks for not asking any questions." He grinned suddenly. "I didn't know David was coming home so early. We must have just missed him."

"No, you didn't," she said. "He saw you go." She

hadn't intended telling him, but the hurt was so deep that she couldn't keep silent.

"What? What do you mean? Did he see Anne and me?"

"Oh, no," Beth answered quietly. "He came up just as you were leaving. He saw you and me instead – and I'm afraid he jumped to certain conclusions."

He gave a low whistle, his face shocked. "Beth, that's awful! Where is he? I'll go and sort it out with him. I can't have him thinking –"

"No. Wait," She held his arm. "Leave it, please, Giles. He'll only think you're making excuses – and besides, I don't want to be the one to let your secret out."

He shook his head. "That's not the point. I can't leave it like that. Good grief! He probably thinks you and I are having an affair!"

"It doesn't matter," she said tonelessly. "Let him think what he likes. No, Giles, leave it, it's too late."

He stood there, fists clenching and unclenching slowly. "Why, the dirty –" He took a deep breath. "I've a good mind to punch him on the nose!"

"And have him even more certain that he was right?" Beth shook her head, the tears not far away. "It doesn't matter, it doesn't matter at all. Come on, let's go back to your aunt." And she smiled, making an effort to seem normal.

He relaxed slightly, and grinned back. "You're wonderful, Beth. Just wonderful. But are you sure –?"

"I'm sure." She walked through the door he held open, her head high, a smile on her lips, and a hollow misery in her heart.

For Mrs. Thornburn's sake she was cheerful for the rest of Christmas afternoon. Fortunately for her, her employer enjoyed the Christmas programmes, so that Beth was free to think her own thoughts at leisure as she pretended to watch.

In the middle of the afternoon, after a light lunch in preparation for the enormous Christmas dinner to be served at seven, they were watching *Little Women*, a perennial Christmas favourite, starring a very youthful Elizabeth Taylor, and June Allyson, when the door opened and David walked in. Beth closed her eyes momentarily, dreading to even look at him, but he too was considering his aunt, apparently, for he said as he entered: "Happy Christmas, ladies," then went to kiss her. Beth stayed very still, fighting for control so that she would be able to speak normally to him. She found that the nails of her hands were digging so hard into the palms that they left marks.

"A happy Christmas to you, my dear," Mrs. Thornburn said, as she embraced him. "I thought a morning in bed, after last night's party, would do you good."

"Very thoughtful of you," he smiled. Then he turned and the smile might never have been. "Will you come to the study for a few moments, Beth? Something has cropped up in a script, and I'd like to sort it out."

"Work! That's all you think of," his aunt grumbled. "Can't it wait a day or so?"

"Well, no. It is rather important, and I know you'll excuse us – we won't be a minute. Beth?" He turned to her, politely waiting, the courteous host attending a guest. It was cleverly done, she thought, as she walked slowly to the door, picking up the walking stick en route, so cleverly done that she could almost have believed it would be about work herself – if she hadn't known better. Her heart began to thud in realization. She was about to have a verbal lashing from that cruel, arrogant tongue. There was a grim set to his jaw as he walked across the hall beside her, in silence. Their footsteps echoed hollowly on the cold floor as they made their way to his study. Beth shivered, suddenly cold. Everything she had ever felt for him had been destroyed last night, when he had said what he had. Beth meant what she had said to Giles – it was too late, in more ways than one. As they went into the study, her doubt hardened into resolve. If he dared to even try and talk to her as he had then, so many hours ago, she would walk out of the house, and never go back.

She turned round to face him as he shut the door behind them.

"Well?" she said. "Tell me why you've bought me here."

He shook his head slowly. "Sit down first, please."

"I'll stand," Beth said, and held her head ever higher. She was ready for him.

He looked down at the carpet for a moment before replying, and she watched him. He had suddenly become like a stranger, a tall remote stranger. He looked at her, and in his eyes was something that caused her heart to stir. Then he spoke.

"Beth, I said certain things to you in this house last night that I had absolutely no right to. I would like to ask your forgiveness." His clear grey eyes met hers, but the glance was no longer hard and direct; it had a waiting quality, a gentleness she had not seen before.

"You implied that I was having an affair with Giles. Am I to take it that you no longer think so?"

"That's not the point," he answered. "It has nothing to do with me."

"You haven't answered my question," Beth said icily.

"Very well. I – don't know."

She moved nearer to him, so that she stood in front of him. She was trembling slightly, and didn't know why, only that she wanted suddenly, to hurt him as much as he'd hurt her. She said slowly:

"Before I accept your apology, I'll tell you something. Two things, as a matter of fact. One – Giles came here about fifteen minutes before you came home. I'm not going to tell you why, because I have been given a confidence that I've no intention of breaking, but I'll tell you now that Giles has never been, or ever will be, anything more than my employer's nephew to me. Secondly – that time you saw me coming out of a cottage with Alan Green. Yes, I'd spent the night there – and I'd slept alone. He gave me the impression that his aunt had invited us both for the weekend, and it wasn't until we actually arrived that I found out he was lying. Yes, he'd hoped to get me into bed with him, and no, he didn't succeed. That was the reason that I finished with him, as a matter of fact – that, and a few other things which have nothing at all to do with you."

Beth took a deep breath, and gripped the walking stick more tightly. Her ankle was hurting like hell, but she hadn't finished. All the pent-up frustration and resentment of the past few months was coming to the surface, and she couldn't have stopped it if she'd tried. "I'll tell you something else, Mr. Benedict. I came here to work as companion-secretary to your aunt, for whom I have the greatest respect and affection. When I found out she hoped I'd work for you as well, I undertook the work gladly – to please her. Since then I've been made to feel your dislike quite plainly. I don't know why you should find me so objectionable. If I've ever done anything to cause your resentment, I'd be glad to know. I've always tried to do my best for you, and I'll tell you why – it was for your aunt's sake, nothing else. She thinks a lot of you, though heaven knows why. I don't. I think you're the most objectionable, unpleasant man I've ever met, and if you ever speak to me like you did, again, I shall leave immediately. As a matter of fact, I was prepared to do just that this afternoon."

She stopped, suddenly appalled by what she had said. The realization came over her in a huge wave as she saw his face, and her legs went weak. Turning, she grabbed desperately at the desk behind her, and leant over it. She was shaking all over, and tears streamed down her face.

She heard movement, and saw David put the chair beside her.

"Sit down," he said, his voice devoid of expression.

Beth did so, quite unable to refuse in any case, and the thought crossed her mind that this was the most awful Christmas Day she had ever spent in her life.

"Have you finished now?" he asked, steely soft.

She nodded, unable to meet those grey eyes. Her answer came in a whisper: "Yes."

Beth heard him let out his breath in a deep sigh, and found the courage to look up. Let him say what he had to, it couldn't be worse than what had gone before, and already the situation was taking on a dream-like quality. She began to feel as if she wasn't really there, as if it wasn't really happening. Any minute, it seemed, she might float away. . . .

"Beth, I didn't realise I'd given you such a terrible impression – and I – Beth, are you listening?"

His voice was getting fainter, and she looked up in alarm. Why was the room going dark too? She held out her hand, and it seemed to waver. She must have called out then, for she heard the cry as everything went black, and the room whirled round her head, mixed with thousands of tiny stars.

Anne was sitting at the bedside when she woke up. Beth looked at her in alarm, remembering the message from Giles.

"Anne," she began, "Giles asked me to tell you to meet him at the usual place, at –" She frowned. She couldn't think what time he had said, nor what she was doing in bed for that matter. "What happened?" she asked, puzzled.

Anne smiled. "You fainted, that's all. And thanks for the message. It'll be the same time as usual, about nine."

"Yes, that's it." Beth was relieved. "B-but how did I get here?"

"Mr. Benedict carried you up. You should have seen his face!" She smiled slightly. "The poor man was white." She smoothed the sheets as if remembering her job, and added: "He's gone to get the doctor now. Old Dr. Longden won't turn out for anyone in this snow, so he's gone to fetch him here."

"Oh," Beth sank back on the pillows, exhausted. She still felt strange, but it was too much effort to ask a lot of questions.

Anne must have sensed this, and said: "Mrs. Thornburn wanted to come up and see you, but he told her to wait until after the doctor had been. I said I'd stay — after all, you helped me last night. Thanks for that, Beth. I'm not used to a lot of drink, and it hit me."

"Giles told me," Beth said slowly. "I like him, he's really nice, and charming."

"I know. I was rather jealous of you at first, when you came," Anne laughed softly. "But he's like that, you know, a bit of a flirt, and it doesn't mean anything."

"He made me feel welcome, Anne. I shall never forget that. I hope everything works out for you."

She patted Beth's arm. "Thanks. I hope so too — but no more talking for a while." She stood up, a tall slim girl who moved with great dignity, and went to open the window slightly. "There, that's better. This central heating's fine, but it does dry the air." She cocked her head, then looked at Beth. "I can hear a car in the distance. I'll bet it's them. He went off like a racing driver."

"Anne," Beth held out her hand towards the girl, "you'll stay with me — while the doctor's here?"

"Of course, if you want me to." She straightened a curtain and looked out across the white expanse surrounding the house. "It gets you, this place. There's something about it. Do you know what I mean?"

"Yes, I know exactly. It feels like home, and yet –"

"And yet it isn't," Anne finished softly. "Yes, I feel like that, too." She sighed suddenly, walking across the thick carpet on silent feet. "I can understand Mr. Benedict – David, I mean, feeling like he does, and working so hard to keep it from the taxman. Sometimes I think he drives himself too hard – but there." She gave a slight shrug. "It's his life, and his choice."

Something in her words made Beth look hard at her. "Anne, what do you mean – what are you saying?"

She turned toward the door, then bit her lip. "They'll be here any minute. I thought you knew. Oh, Beth, I wouldn't have said anything, but I assumed he'd told you why –"

"Anne, tell me, please." Beth grabbed her hand. "Quickly!"

Again that swift glance toward the door, then she sat down on the bed, and spoke very quietly. "It's all to do with death duties. Giles told me a while ago. David's father died three or four years ago, and the death duties were absolutely fantastic – hundreds of thousands of pounds. It left the estate virtually penniless, and if it hadn't been for David's work – he gets lots of money for every script, you know – the whole place would have had to be sold to break even, or given to the Government, or something perfectly awful. David said something like, 'over my dead body,' and set to, and sold some priceless family heirlooms, and paintings, and started producing T.V. plays right, left and centre. He's a marvel really, I don't know how he

106

does it. He was already writing for television, but on a smaller scale."

Beth lay back weakly, and closed her eyes. "But — Mrs. Thornburn told me he did it more or less as a hobby — she was most emphatic that he didn't need the money."

Anne laughed softly. "I know. Giles says she's living in the past as far as finance is concerned. She honestly doesn't realise what it takes to run a place this size, and David won't give her any worry at all. She potters about doing her charity work, and she's happy — but if she only *knew*!" She stood up. "Ssh, they're here." Beth could hear the footsteps on the stairs, only faintly, and voices. Her mind was still in a whirl. At last she knew why David wrote as he did, frantically and ceaselessly. Even now, after his behaviour, it aroused a spark of admiration for his single-mindedness. He must have a fierce love for his home, and his work was an achievement to be proud of.

She looked toward the door as, after a brief knock, the old doctor came in alone.

Beth had her Christmas dinner in bed, so she was spared the ordeal of eating it with David downstairs. Two days in bed was the doctor's main prescription for what turned out to be delayed shock following her fall in the snow. He had glared at her suspiciously from under thick brows.

"And what have you been up to, eh, miss?" he demanded. "Dragging me away from ma pipe and ma turkey on a Christmas Day? It had better be good."

"I'm sorry, Doctor. I didn't intend to be any trouble. I didn't even know Mr. Benedict had gone for you. Apparently I fainted."

"Hmph! You girls and your slimming – not eating enough, that's what it is. Nothing much wrong with you." He pulled down Beth's bottom eyelid. "Ah, hmm, a wee bit anaemic too. Well, we'll soon put that right." He began to shake out some red capsules into a box. She didn't dare to tell him that she wouldn't dream of slimming. No one argued with Dr. Longden, ever. She accepted his mild rebuke, smiled and thanked him, and watched him go with a feeling of relief.

Anne brought her up her dinner. "You'll be pleased to know," she said as she plumped the pillows, "that the dear doctor was driven home by David with the best part of a bottle of good Scotch under his waistcoat." She giggled. "I bet he stopped telling David off after the third glass!"

"He told *David* off," Beth whispered, unbelieving.

She nodded. "Not half! Said he thought you were dying, the way David told it – and he finds you pink and pretty and not much at all wrong."

"I feel awful about it," Beth said wretchedly.

"It's not your fault," Anne answered. "Get on with your turkey. It's delicious. Do you want me to stay with you until you've finished it?"

"No, I'm all right, I don't want you to be late for Giles," Beth answered.

"It's all right – he'll wait. It'll do him good, anyway. Serve him right for getting me tiddly last night." She sat back and clasped her hands behind her head. "No,

I take that back. It was my fault as much as his. And he's super really, Beth. If only —"

"His mother?" Beth asked, tentatively.

"Mmm, yes. You've met her. I don't need to tell you, do I?" Anne sighed deeply. "That's his own fault. I love him dearly, but one of us has got to be sensible about this. I won't run away and have a hole in the corner wedding in some poky register office. I intend to be married in the village church or nothing. And he's got to be the one to tell his mother. No one else can do it for him."

"She is pretty formidable," Beth agreed.

"She is, but I'm not afraid of her, you know. I'd tell her tomorrow if I had to — but he's got to do it. It must be done properly — I'll not have a bitch like her saying I 'stole' her son." She turned and looked at Beth, her pale clear eyes calm and wise, and Beth thought that if anyone could deal with Rose, it was Anne. Gentle as she was, there was a hard core of strength about her that would not allow anyone to bully her. Beth wished them well in her heart of hearts. Anne was a girl who knew what she wanted — and Beth didn't doubt that she'd get it. And what did Beth want? She didn't even know.

Mrs. Thornburn came up to see Beth after she had eaten, and was reading. She brought with her a small gift-wrapped package.

"My dear," she began, "I completely forgot your Christmas present. And thank you so much for yours — but you shouldn't have, you know."

It was a heavy chain bracelet, filled with charms, old gold in colour, and beautifully designed. Beth thanked her delightedly, but she tut-tutted. "Nonsense! It's an old one of mine as a matter of fact, and you've got such slim, pretty wrists – it'll look much better on you."

Beth looked down at it in dismay. "Mrs. Thornburn, you don't mean – it's not – I mean, it's gold!"

"Why, yes!" She seemed surprised. "You do like it?"

"But you can't," Beth said, a warm tide of colour surging up her cheeks. "Please, I can't accept –"

"Of course you can. Heavens, was that all that was bothering you? My dear child, nothing would give me greater pleasure than to see you wearing it. As a matter of fact, it was Great-Uncle Rufus who gave it to me on my twenty-first birthday, so it probably has quite a history, like him." And she burst into delighted laughter. She refused to listen to any more protests, and as she left, said: "Oh, yes, I nearly forgot. I'll send David up with the phone. I'm sure you'd love to call your mother today."

"Please tell him not to bother," Beth began – but Mrs. Thornburn was already out of the room, and she sank back wearily. What was the use? It would be nice to phone her mother, of course, although she would never be able to tell her of the day's dreadful events. She'd think Beth was having a lovely time, with perhaps even a kiss under the mistletoe from that marvellous man, Mr. Benedict. If only she knew! But no one could ever know Beth's dreadful, humiliating experience; that was something she had to bear entirely alone.

The knock came soon afterwards, firm and light, and she called:

"Come in."

David walked in, carrying a red phone. Instantly the room was filled with electric tension, crackling round them, so that Beth was almost suffocating. She took a deep breath, and prayed he would go away. Surely he wasn't so insensitive – couldn't he feel it?

"Aunt Lavinia asked me to bring this for you," he said, going and kneeling by the bedside, where he plugged it into a socket in the skirting board. She had wondered what that was for; now she knew.

"Thank you."

He stood by the bed. "How do you feel?"

"Very well, thank you," Beth answered, her voice stiff and harsh. "And now, if you don't mind, I'm rather tired –" she looked pointedly at the door.

"Yes, I'm going. Before I do, though, one thing I must finish. I made you an apology. Have you accepted it?"

"All right." Beth looked into his grey eyes. "Perhaps we both said things that are best forgotten. I don't think you'll have any more opportunities to jump to the wrong conclusions – I'll make sure of that. After all, this is your house, and I am only an employee. Don't worry, Mr. Benedict, I'll never forget my position again." She was breathless when she had finished.

"Don't. Don't talk like that," he said. He shook his head. "If you knew how badly I felt about it. You did right to hit me, I deserved it. You should have punched me on the nose –"

"Yes," Beth said, stupidly, not realising, "that's what Giles said when I told –" She stopped, appalled, as his face changed. There was a dreadful silence, as he closed his eyes, then, opening them, looked at her. They were dark with a frightening kind of anger, but his voice was strangely quiet as he said: "Dear God, what a fool I've been!" He moved away as if frightened what he might do. "And to think I believed you!" His contempt lashed her as he went on, "I'll bet you couldn't wait to tell him, could you?"

Stunned with shock at his reaction, knowing with dreadful clarity what must be going on in his mind, Beth said, shakenly: "Wait, you don't understand, I –"

"Perhaps I don't, nor do I want to." Without another word, he turned on his heel and walked out, tall, stiff-backed.

She lay there in utter misery as the tears welled up unbidden, and, unable to stop them, she wept.

CHAPTER SIX

The events of that Christmas Day became a shadow affecting Beth's life from then on at Benedict House. She was determined not to tell either Giles or Anne what had happened. They had enough problems of their own, and Anne often told her about the difficulties, on their rare chances to chat. Giles was working hard to get enough money to become financially independent of his mother, who had virtually held the purse strings until only recently, for it wasn't until his twenty-fifth birthday that money from a trust fund had come to him, and it was tied up securely in stocks and shares. He wanted to avoid touching that, and instead worked hard on the farms that belonged to the Benedict estate. Soon, they hoped, they would be able to get married. It was obvious to Beth that they were deeply in love, and what was surprising was that no one else could see it, especially Rose Benedict, whose eyes and ears were extremely keen, and missed little. It wasn't odd that David didn't see, for he practically lived in his own study.

Ever since that dreadful evening, he had changed. Even Mrs. Thornburn was worried about him. "I've never seen David like this before," she confided in Beth one February morning as they drove to Buxton. She was glad of these occasional trips out, for work was now difficult, with the atmosphere that existed. He was remoter than ever, a stranger who drove himself on, working night and day writing. Beth avoided going to London at the same time as him, because she couldn't bear the thought of sitting next to him for several hours. His mother was puzzled about it, but Beth fobbed her off with excuses, for she couldn't even talk about him. For one thing she had discovered, painfully, since Christmas, she was still in love with him. The love she had thought destroyed by his words, and that searing, cruel kiss, had merely been dormant. It was torture to see him every day, to speak to him, to hear him, and all about work, and scripts.

Beth answered Mrs. Thornburn now, keeping her eyes carefully on the road ahead. "What do you mean?" she asked.

"So busy. He's driving himself harder than I've ever seen him, Beth. Can't you do something, make him ease up a bit?"

"I don't think he'd listen to me," Beth answered, trying to speak casually, but unable to keep a tremor out of her voice.

"But the work – all that typing," she insisted. "Heavens, it's too much for you, my dear. You know, I don't want you getting ill with overwork as well."

"Didn't he tell you?" Beth said, surprised. "He's started sending odd scripts to the typing agency again. It leaves me freer to do more letters, you see."

"He tells me nothing," his aunt said sadly. "Oh, I'm worried about him, I don't mind telling you. He can't go on like this without cracking up eventually."

"Perhaps if he went away for a holiday? Why don't you persuade him?" Beth suggested. Outwardly casual, inside she ached with worry too, but she had to keep hers hidden.

"Mmm, yes," Mrs. Thornburn said thoughtfully. "I can try. You're going home for a week soon, aren't you? Perhaps he'll go to Paris, at the same time."

"Perhaps," Beth agreed. Secretly she doubted it. Reluctantly, and only after much heart-searching, she was coming to the conclusion that she would soon have to leave. It wouldn't be running away, she knew that, for deep inside she sensed that David Benedict would not drive himself so hard if she wasn't there. She had no tangible reason for this knowledge, it was more an instinct, deep-rooted and immovable. If she went, it would be better for everyone, herself included. Beth knew she would be letting Mrs. Thornburn down, and this was the only thing that gave her pause, but she knew too that she couldn't carry on much longer like this, working for a cold stranger, one with violence smouldering just below the surface, like a slumbering volcano that might erupt at any time.

It was two days later, a Friday, that it happened. The day began normally enough, if normal was the word for the conditions under which Beth now worked. She had two scripts on the desk, and began one at nine a.m. promptly, hoping she would get it finished by lunch. It was already three-quarters done, and she hoped to be off early that afternoon to go home for the weekend. She typed quickly away, broke for coffee at eleven and started again ten minutes later. She left the script piled neatly beside her typewriter when she went for lunch, intending to go through and check it afterwards.

When Beth returned, it had gone. She stood by the desk for a moment wondering, when the door to David's study opened and he came in. She knew at once that he was in a temper by the way he brandished the missing script in his hand.

"I was looking for that –" Beth began.

"I thought you were a secretary," he said, flicking the pages contemptuously. "This script is full of mistakes."

"Mistakes?" she echoed. "But I haven't been through it yet. I always –"

"I wanted it finished by lunch," he interrupted. "I told you that yesterday morning. I particularly want this to go off today. It'll take hours to correct."

Beth tried to keep her voice calm. "I think that's an exaggeration," she answered. "It usually only takes half an hour. If you'll give the script to me," she held out her hand, "I'll do it now."

He handed the bulky pile of papers to her, and Beth glanced down the top page. He would have to pick this one, off all those she had done! There were several glaring, stupid errors on it, and they surprised her. She turned the sheet, frowning. The next page had a couple of errors, simple ones that could be easily put right. She looked up. "I'll retype this first sheet," she said. "I do seem to have made a few more mistakes than usual, but –"

"Perhaps I'd better start checking them all again," he said, before Beth could finish. "I thought you were accurate, however –" this with a shrug, and a significant pause as he looked again at the papers. She put them down on the table. Her patience and temper were both wearing thin, and she said, without thinking: "If I was given a little more time to do them, instead of having to work at breakneck speed –"

"You mean you can't cope?" he demanded sarcastically. "Perhaps you'd like me to get another secretary as well as you?"

"I doubt," Beth said icily, "if anyone else would put up with your temper, or your rudeness. You haven't let me finish a sentence yet! If you'd allowed me, I was going to say that it's difficult to be completely accurate at the best of times. With you breathing down my neck, it's virtually impossible!" She felt her cheeks flush, and knew that she was glaring at him, unable to help herself.

"What you mean is that you're in a desperate hurry to get your train to London, and so the work suffers," he said infuriatingly.

"If you like – anything to get away from *you*," Beth retorted. "And now I'll get on with correcting my mistakes, if you don't mind." She sat down abruptly and picked up the paper.

"And when you've done that, you can begin this other script," he said.

She looked up. "I intend doing so." She was trying to keep calm, trying so hard to keep her temper from boiling over. She knew the pressures under which he worked, and though she had some understanding of his behaviour, there was a limit to what she could take from him. Beth too had her problems, but there was no one

117

who could help her. She had to try and control the agony of working near him, living in close proximity, and keeping up an impersonal front. If it hadn't been for Mrs. Thornburn, she would have given up long ago. As it was, even she, living in her pleasant world, sensed that Beth wasn't happy, and characteristically she blamed herself.

"I'm making you do too much," she'd say, as Beth drove her to a friend's house on the alternate weekends when she didn't go home, and Beth would protest that she enjoyed helping her very much, but she would remain unconvinced. How could she be so blind? Beth would have done anything for her, but she wasn't the problem, her nephew David was.

Now, deliberately ignoring the furious man who stood by her desk, Beth bent to her task, and began to retype the first page. He was watching her. She wondered why. Why was he standing there so silently? Pressing her lips firmly together, she typed determinedly on, trying to ignore him. But it was impossible. Why wouldn't he go away? She would finish much quicker.

In sudden exasperation she looked up, and started to speak, then stopped. She had surprised such an expression of utter torment on his face that she almost gasped. It was frightening to see – a moment later it was gone, and might never have been, as he said with heavy irony: "I see that I distract you. Excuse me." He went out, closing his study door firmly behind him. Beth stared at the heavy oak door, blank and uncompromising, for several puzzled seconds, in the silence that hung after his words. She saw again that expression, and wondered at it. Why, oh, why? she asked herself. But she knew no answer. Unless it was that David Benedict had reached the point where he was about to have a breakdown. And the awful thing was, there was nothing she could do about it, nothing at all.

Beth looked again at the typewriter before her, and the paper blurred and wavered in front of her eyes. She too was tired, because she couldn't sleep at nights, and she had lost weight. It would be a relief to be at home for two nights, but it passed so quickly, and in no time she would be back at Benedict House, to start another week.

She resolved there and then that it couldn't go on for much longer. In the spring she would tell Mrs. Thornburn that she was going to leave. She would let her know in good time. It might take one or two months to find a replacement. Beth had no intention of leaving either of them in the lurch. But they would find someone, and when they did she would be free to go. And she would never allow herself to fall in love again. There was no joy in it, none at all. Only pain, and disillusion.

"You've changed these last few months," Beth's mother said, watching her as she sat down to dinner on the Friday night. She looked up from the delicious steak and kidney pie, and smiled, trying to make light of her remark.

"So have you," Beth answered. "Your cooking's improved, and you look years younger since you went to work at that office. Er – there wouldn't be a good-looking man working there, by any chance?"

Judith looked up grinning from the chair where she sprawled, reading a pop star magazine. "Careful, Beth, you're treading on thin ice!"

"What?" She whirled back to her mother, whose cheeks had gone slightly pink, and who had suddenly become busy plumping up cushions, as she answered: "Don't talk nonsense, Judith." Then to Beth, "And don't try to change the subject! It's you we're talking about. What are they doing to you at that place? You've no colour in your cheeks at all. Country air like that, why you should be rosy – and aren't you eating?"

"Of course, Mum. It's just that Mr. – David's terribly busy at the moment. He's even started sending scripts to the agency again, because he gets lots of letters, and he doesn't want me overworked."

"Hmmm," her mother snorted, though slightly mollified. "Too busy to give you any lifts any more, I suppose?"

Beth bent her head to her plate and started eating again. Her mother meant well. She just didn't realise how painfully close she was to making Beth cry. That was something else she couldn't understand about herself just lately. It was no use. She would have to confide in someone, or go mad. And then she remembered Anne.

Beth told her late on Sunday night what she had decided. They were in her room, and Anne had come up to see the trouser suit she had bought during her weekend at home.

She sat on the bed looking with a critical eye as Beth swept across the carpet in the best Dior manner.

"Like it?"

She nodded enthusiastically. "Yes, Beth. That dark blue really suits you, makes your hair almost ash-blonde." She sighed. "Lucky you! Why wasn't I born beautiful?"

Beth began to laugh. "Anne, you are an idiot! You've got a lovely face – oh, I see, you were just fishing for compliments!"

Anne smiled. "No, I wasn't. You are very attractive, Beth. But I don't think you need me to tell you."

Beth took off the jacket and put it carefully on the bed. "Thank you." She looked at the other girl sitting there so calmly and serenely, and it was her turn to sigh. "It must be nice having a man to take you places. I could do with a good night out."

Anne opened her eyes wide. "That's an idea! We could –"

"Whoa, just a second!" Beth said weakly. "I was only joking –"

"So? An evening out would do you good. You work too hard for that unappreciative swine!"

"Anne!" Beth was shocked by her choice of words.

The other girl looked up, an impish smile on her face. "Well, it's true. Giles says he wants shaking. He told me what happened that night – you know – Christmas Eve, and –"

"No," Beth said quickly. "Let's forget it." She shook her head. "That's best forgotten." She bit her lip, then said: "Anne, I might as well tell you now. I'm going to leave soon."

"What!" Anne nearly dropped the jacket of the

121

trouser suit that she had been examining. "When? Have you told him?"

"No. I'll tell Mrs. Thornburn first – after all, she is my employer, officially."

"Beth, is it because of what happened – you know, at Christmas?"

"Partly, I suppose." She looked at Anne, then said hesitantly: "I'm sure I can tell you, in confidence, of course."

"You can," Anne answered quietly. "I won't even tell Giles." She smiled. "I can keep secrets."

"Yes, I know. Well, it's quite simple." Beth sat down beside her, absentmindedly moving the new jacket to one side. "I've had the misfortune to fall in l-love with David Benedict." Her lip trembled, and she paused for a moment, then went on: "You can tell me I'm mad – though I already know it – but it's unbearable, working with him. He's impossible, and he's getting worse. I don't mean the amount of work, I can cope with that, but it's his manner – and he h-hates me." Shaking, Beth reached for her hanky and blew her nose. But she felt a strong feeling of relief at having it out at last.

"Oh, Beth!" Anne's arm came round her shoulder, warm and sympathetic. "You poor thing. I didn't guess! I thought –" she stopped.

"You thought what?" Beth sniffed.

"Well, you seemed so super-efficient and cool – I thought you'd got him nicely sorted out. Oh, Beth, I'm so sorry. It's hell when you love someone, and they're unpleasant to you." She looked thoughtfully at her. "It's strange, you know, he never used to be like he is.

I mean he worked hard, of course, and he used to drive Miss Whatsit round the bend sometimes, but she worshipped him, in the nicest possible way. And he was always courteous. In fact," she nodded slowly, "in fact, to be quite honest, I don't think I've ever seen him like he is now."

"Well, I can't take much more from him," Beth said, more calmly. "It's affecting my work. I'm making mistakes, and I used to be so accurate. He blew up at me on Friday, implied I was hopeless. That was when I decided I couldn't take much more."

"Mmm, Friday. Yes, he even had a row with Mrs. Thornburn in the evening, I could hear them when I passed the library – perhaps he wasn't feeling well. You know what men are if they've only got something like a headache; like grouchy bears."

"He had a row with his aunt? That's awful! "

"And unusual. But he apologised afterwards. I'll say one thing in his favour, he really thinks the world of her. She's been like a second mother to him ever since his own left."

"Left? I imagined her to be dead."

"She is now," Anne answered. "But she left his father when David was only about twelve. Ran away with the chauffeur – yes, it sounds like a corny old movie, but it happened. And his father never married again."

"I didn't know," Beth said.

Anne looked at her oddly. "There's a lot you don't know about David Benedict," she said. "He's not had it easy. I know it doesn't excuse his behaviour to you, but sometimes – well," she shrugged, "it helps to explain it."

"Yes, I suppose so. Thanks for listening to me, Anne. You've helped a lot. I'm a selfish thing, aren't I? Going on about my problems when you've got your own."

"That's what friends are for – and we are friends, I hope?"

"I hope so too. Can we write to each other when I go? I'd like to hear how you get on."

"Of course." Anne stood up and looked at her watch. "Heavens, it's nearly midnight! I'd better go." She walked to the door, turned the handle, hesitated, then walked slowly back. "Just one thing before I go," she said. "It's been at the back of my mind ever since I saw your face when you were telling me. It's this." She smiled a strange little smile. "I've thought for ages that David was in love with you. I realise now that I was mistaken. But it's something I've been unable to forget, the way I saw him watching you one night when you were at dinner. He looked like a man in torment. As though – as though he wanted to grab you, and – oh, I don't know – still, after what you've told me tonight, I'd better forget it." She turned away. " 'Night, Beth. Things will seem better in the morning."

Beth hardly heard the words, or saw her leave. A man in torment. It reminded her of the look she had surprised on his face that dreadful Friday lunchtime two days ago. She shivered, suddenly cold.

Perhaps because her mind was made up, and she knew she would be leaving before much longer, the situation seemed to improve slightly in the following few days. At the back of Beth's mind was a dull kind of sadness at her decision, but there was no alternative, and at least she wasn't rushing into it, as she had with Alan. She would miss the house, she knew that already. It had taken hold of her more than she had ever thought possible. It was but stone and mortar after all, inanimate, yet filled with an atmosphere of life and love. It had been built in the eighteenth century and passed down through generations of Benedicts with love and care. And each generation of the family had left their mark on it, from the very first, who had probably watched the tender shoots of ivy make their precarious way from the ground, inches at a time, the ivy that now smothered the grey walls in thick profusion, to David himself, the latest of the line, who had installed central heating the year before his father's death. It was hard to imagine what the bedrooms could have been like, before that, in winter.

Beth looked out across the gardens, so impeccably kept by George and his brother. In the distance she could see a small figure bending over one of the stone lions that guarded steps down to a sunken rose garden, and smiled to herself as she recognised Christine, the child from the village. Even in winter there were jobs to be done. Even when the place was grey and uninteresting, there was life deep beneath the ground, quivering life as the seeds awaited the coming of spring, and warmth. And perhaps, when the garden was at its best, she would be gone. Her throat constricted at the thought.

Soon she would tell Mrs. Thornburn. All the time she

remained here, knowing she wanted to leave, and without her employer's knowledge, made her feel as if she was living a lie. Beth resolved there and then to tell her at the first opportunity. One evening when there was just the two of them, and Beth could perhaps begin, if only slightly, to make her see her reasons. For she knew she could not tell her less than the truth. Beth disliked lies and evasions; with a woman as wonderful as Mrs. Thornburn, anything else would be unthinkable.

The week went quickly by, and the opportunity didn't arise. An old friend of Mrs. Thornburn came to stay for a few days, and Beth was left to her own devices in the evenings. On Sunday afternoon Anne caught up with her as she walked down to the gate, for a stroll.

"Beth," she took hold of her arm, "I was looking for you."

"Hello. I came out for a breath of air. Mrs. Thornburn and Lady Summerfield are gossiping about old times, and it got a bit boring, so I came out."

"Yes, Lady S. does go on a bit, doesn't she? Anyway, what I wanted to tell you was this. You're free tonight?"

"Yes. Always at weekends. Why?"

"Would you like to come out with Giles and me this evening?"

"Oh! It's good of you – but –"

"No buts!" Anne said firmly. "We want to thank you for all the help you've given us."

"Thanks, Anne," Beth smiled. "Yes, I'd love to. What time?"

"About eight-thirty. Don't eat, we're going for a meal."

"I'll try. Oh, yes. Who do I tell Mrs. Thornburn I'm going out with? You know, do I imply that you've got a boy-friend, or not?"

Anne laughed. "It's all right. She knows I'm going out with someone, but she thinks he lives in Buxton. It's not nice to deceive her, I know, and she never asks questions anyway, but if she did find out, she might think it was her duty to tell you-know-who, and we've already been into that, haven't we?"

"Point taken," Beth answered. "I'll just say I'm going out with you. Where will we meet Giles?"

"I'll show you. Must dash now. Mum's making some fantastic concoction for our titled guest's sweet tonight – and she says that if she turns up her nose at this one she'll take great delight in upending it over her ladyship's head!" As she sped away, she said in answer to Beth's hasty question: "It's a lemon mousse!"

Beth was still laughing as she reached the gate. Anne did her good. For all her cool exterior, the girl had a lively sense of humour, and a fascinating personality. It was easy to see why Giles loved her.

"Hello, Miss."

Startled by the voice, Beth turned quickly to see the girl from the village, Christine Newton, crossing the road towards her. She had seen her several times since their first accidental meeting, but she always seemed in a hurry, and had only time for a brief wave before vanishing. Beth had decided that the child was frightened she might take her home if she stopped!

"Hello," Beth answered. "Where are you off to?"

Christine lifted her shoulders in a very adult shrug.

"Somewhere, a walk." She was dressed in the inevitable blue anorak and red wellingtons. Her hair had grown slightly, and was tied with elastic bands into two clumps.

"Can I come?" Beth asked, and saw her surprise, then she smiled. There was something appealing about her, and a spirit of adventure shone out through the dirty, rosy-cheeked face. Small and young as she was, Beth sensed that she would grow up into an interesting woman. Christine held out her hand, after that momentary hesitation. "C'mon then." Just as she began to lead Beth off, she paused. "Er, you won't tell anyone about where I'm taking you, will you?" Beth looked suspiciously at her. Was it somewhere on private property? she wondered. Christine guessed her thoughts, for she gave a gap-toothed grin and added: "S'all right, only it's *my* secret place, and I've never shown anyone before." Beth nodded, and put a suitably impressed expression on her face, and they set off.

In the next two hours, Beth heard her complete life story. She spoke naturally and unselfconsciously, and through it all, the grumbles and grouses about her home, her parents and the school she unwillingly attended, came the deep love of life, and the country.

There was something else, too; her devotion to her family. A wanderer she might be, but it certainly wasn't because she was neglected, Beth felt sure. It was simply that the spirit of adventure was too great to be contained in her sturdy little frame.

"I'm going to be a mountaineer," she said as they sat on a rather damp flat rock on top of a hill. They were in her 'secret place,' and now Beth knew why she so often appeared near Benedict House. It was on her route there. Behind them as they sat was a small cave, well concealed by rocks. She had taken Beth in when they first arrived, and proudly shown her the wooden box covered with an old blanket that was her little camping seat. Beth smiled, and admired it, and secretly wondered at her imagination.

Now, as they sat outside, Beth looked down at the rolling countryside below them, and drank it all in. She could see Benedict House far away to her left, gracious and perfect, even from this distance, dominating the surroundings. And with the trees, stone walls, different shades of green in the fields, the whole panorama was like a giant patchwork quilt. And so beautiful, so very beautiful. She could scarcely believe that she had once imagined Derbyshire to be bleak and uninteresting.

She wrenched herself back to the present as Christine repeated her words, and answered quickly: "A mountaineer? It sounds very interesting, but I think you'll find it hard work."

"Have you ever done any?" the child demanded in her direct manner.

"Well, no," Beth had to admit. "But I've seen it on T.V., and it seems very tricky."

"Well, I'm going to a school to *learn* it when I'm big enough. There's one near Buxton. And I'm going to join a mountain rescue team, and help people who get stuck. I'm not stopping at silly school till I'm sixteen."

"Oh, Christine," Beth sighed. "You'll have to wait until you're much older. In the meantime it would be a big help if you learned all your lessons at school. They

129

won't have mountain rescuers who can't read or write, you know."

The child considered her thoughtfully. It was obvious that this aspect had not occurred to her before. Eventually she said: "Are you sure?"

"Positive," Beth answered firmly. "Why, I'll bet you even have to pass tests before you can join the mountaineers, just to prove that you're bright enough to know what to do in an emergency."

Christine jumped up. "Right! Come on, let's go back. And you can test me now on spelling. I'm very good at spelling, you know. So give me some words. Not too long, just nice ones." She held out her hand, and as Beth racked her brains for nice, not too long words, they began the downward walk home.

CHAPTER SEVEN

At three o'clock the following morning, Anne, Giles, and Beth stood shivering in the cold night air while Giles fumbled to open the back door to the kitchens of Benedict House.

He swore softly, and Anne and Beth clung, giggling helplessly, to each other.

"Ssh, don't make a noise!" he ordered in mild exasperation. "Do you want to wake everyone up?"

That sobered them. They stood perfectly still, hands to mouths, listening to the rattling of the key in the lock. Then – "Ah, that's it." With a deft twist of the key, he opened the door with a flourish, and handed back the key to Anne.

"Are you coming in for a coffee?" she whispered. He shook his head, and bent to kiss her. "No, my love. Just in case David's still up. In you go. Lock the door now."

" 'Bye, darling," Anne whispered. "Be careful going down the drive." She listened until his footsteps died away, then locked the door firmly, and leaned against it. "Oh, what a night!" She looked across at Beth as she poured water into a pan. "Did you enjoy it, Beth?"

"It was marvellous. I'm going to have a cup of coffee before I go to bed. You'll have one?"

"Yes, please." She sat down carefully at the kitchen table.

"Are you going home this weekend?"

"Yes, I think so. I'm also going to tell Mrs. Thornburn about leaving before I go."

"Oh, Beth, don't do it unless you're sure. I mean, I thought things had improved slightly this week."

Beth laughed as she poured the boiling water on to the instant coffee that Anne had put into cups. "Things have been slightly better this week, but only because I've had as little to do with David as possible, and also, I think, because I've made up my mind."

Anne nodded slowly. "Perhaps. Oh, but he wants shaking!"

"Don't you start," Beth protested. "He's a law unto himself. Nothing will change him. I don't even want to try, not any more." And she lifted her cup, and drank the coffee slowly.

For the first time in ages, she slept soundly that night.

Beth had barely started work the next morning, when David entered the room

"Can I help you?" Beth asked.

"Yes. When you've finished that page, I'd like you to take some dictation. Come into my study."

"Yes, Mr. Benedict." Beth turned away and began to type again. Why, how, did he make her feel so guilty, and somehow cheap, just by the way he looked at her? This was how it was now; almost unbearable, feeling as she did. She knew she mustn't delay telling first Mrs. Thornburn, and then him. Once it was done, she would feel freer. It was to happen sooner than she expected, within minutes, in fact.

Beth went in and sat down opposite his desk, her note pad open, pen at the ready. "Right, sir." She knew he hated her calling him sir. He had never said so in so many words, but the tightening of his jaw muscles was enough to give him away. Now, this morning, he must have decided to speak.

"Miss Kendrick," he began, "I prefer you not to call me 'sir.' It's an outdated, old-fashioned word. If you cannot bring yourself to call me by my name, I would rather have none at all."

"Very well, s – Mr. Benedict," Beth said, trying not to smile. Something had rattled him, anyway. She decided to find out what it was. "Mr. Benedict," she said, "I'm sorry if I've annoyed you. I'll try and see that it doesn't happen again."

He shrugged, clearly unconcerned. Then he bent and picked up a calendar from the desk. "By the way, when do you want your holidays?"

Beth felt the colour drain from her face. How could she answer?

"I d-don't know," she stammered.

He looked at her oddly. "What's the matter? Aren't you well?"

"I – yes," she nodded slowly. "It's just that – I don't know," she repeated lamely. She was aware that he was watching her, frowning, and her face flamed. It was no use. He suspected something, and if she kept silent it would be cowardly. So now was the moment.

Quickly, without allowing herself to analyse too deeply what she was about to do, Beth said: "I won't need

133

any holidays. I intend to leave as soon as you can find a replacement. You took me by surprise, because I wanted to tell Mrs. Thornburn, your aunt, tonight. It's only fair that I tell her first, because she is my employer, after all."

Then she looked up at him, not knowing what he would be like. She expected anger, perhaps sarcasm. She didn't expect him to look as he did; completely blank, as if shutters had closed. Then, after the silence grew taut, he spoke, his voice controlled and even.

"Thank you for telling me," he said. "You'd better go back to the script."

"But I came in for dictation!" Beth said. There was a hard knot of pain in her stomach. What she had known all along was proved. He didn't care a damn one way or another. Not even at losing a secretary. If ever she had cherished the slightest, smallest hope about him, it was gone in the face of that calm indifference.

"The letters don't matter. I've changed my mind," he answered. And he turned his back on her and went to the window. She looked at him standing there, and stood up, smoothing her skirt as she did so. He didn't move, a tall broad-shouldered man sharply outlined in the cold clear light from outside. Quietly, Beth made her way to the door and went back into her own office.

"But, my dear, I don't know what to say! I'm completely shattered. Oh, child, I thought you were happy here!"

They were in Mrs. Thornburn's large bedroom, next

134

to Beth's own, and it was afternoon. Lady Summerfield
had gone to have her usual post-lunch rest, and Beth
had seized her chance as they left the dining room, and
asked Mrs. Thornburn if she could have a private word
with her. Puzzled, she had told Beth to go to her room,
where she was going to change. Now, as she sat in the
hard-backed chair by Mrs. Thornburn's window, the
old lady turned slightly from her seat at the dressing
table, where she sat choosing earrings to wear that night,
and said, with sudden shrewdness: "Beth, I feel that
I know you as well as if you were my own daughter.
So what I'm going to say is perfectly frank – and I hope
you'll do me the favour of answering with equal honesty."

Beth nodded slightly. "Yes, I will."

"Then I'll ask you first. Is your reason for leaving
connected with either of my two nephews?"

Beth's lips were dry, and she passed her tongue quickly
over them. Very quietly, she said: "Yes."

"Is it Giles?"

"No."

"Ah!" The old lady let out her breath in an audible
sigh. "I should have known. Do you love him?"

"I –" Beth's heart beat faster, but she had to answer. "Yes," she said, her voice barely a whisper. "And
he – he – not only is he completely indifferent, I could
cope with that, b-but he dislikes me. He's barely civil
most of the time." She stopped, aghast. "I'm sorry. You
asked for frankness, but I have no right to criticize a
relative –"

Mrs. Thornburn held up a hand. "No, you have

every right. And I'll admit it, what you say intrigues me. It will go no further than this room, I promise. What do you mean, barely civil? Is he actually rude or insulting to you?" Her face reflected her honest bewilderment, and Beth hastened to answer.

"No, it's not like that. I'm putting it very badly, Mrs. Thornburn. He – oh, I don't know – there's just an awful atmosphere when we're working together, a tension that I can't do anything to dispel. I'm sure he must be aware of it, in fact, I think he's changed even since I've been working for him. He drives himself too hard, and there are times when I actually dread having to ask him anything."

Mrs. Thornburn nodded, her faded blue eyes shrewd. "Yes, you're quite right. I too have noticed this change in him. And you have no idea why it could be?"

"No." Beth was uneasily aware that Mrs. Thornburn was watching her closely, and she turned more to face her. "No, none at all. Have you?"

She smiled so slightly that it was gone even as Beth saw it. "I don't know," she answered. "I'm not sure. Oh, how blind he must be! The Benedict men have always been foolish, in need of guidance. I didn't guess that David would follow suit." She held up a pair of dainty filigree earrings to the light, where they glinted and glittered in the faint movement of the air. Her eyes were kind as she said: "And it must be painful, feeling as you do about him. I quite understand your desire to leave, even though I must say that I don't want you to go. I find you delightful company – but then I'm a selfish old woman."

136

"No, never that." Beth reached out to touch her hand. "You're most wonderful and unselfish. I feel so badly about even asking you to accept my resignation. But my position is becoming impossible, and quite frankly I can't see it getting any better."

"Have you told David?" the old lady asked casually, not looking at Beth, riffling through a trinket box with idle fingers.

"Yes. I intended telling you first, naturally, but it came out when he asked me about holidays."

"And what did he say? Was he surprised, dismayed?"

Beth shook her head. "No. It was just as though nothing had happened. He thanked me for telling him, and told me to go back to work."

The old lady tightened her mouth. "Yes, he would. I thought you'd say that. It's the Benedict men all over, stiff-necked and idiotic." She suddenly flung the earrings back into the box. "Oh, my child, if only I could help you!"

"You can't. Nobody can. I'll get over it, when I'm away from here. And that's why I have to go." Beth stood up. "I think I'd better go down now. I'll be late back from lunch, and I have a lot to do. Thank you for listening."

Mrs. Thornburn said nothing, only shook her head, as if unable to speak.

Now she knew. Now it was official.

It was obvious that some kind of conference had taken place when, returning later that evening from a walk round the grounds after dinner, Beth entered the lounge. There she found David and his aunt awaiting her. Mrs. Thornburn sat in the middle of her huge settee, David was standing by the fireplace.

"Have a drink?" he asked, as Beth sat beside Mrs. Thornburn.

"Yes, do, my dear," she said. "A drop of brandy will warm you up. You look frozen from being outside. Yes, David, Beth will have a brandy."

Beth thanked him for the glass of clear golden liquid that he handed to her, and drank, gasping a little as the warmth crept down her throat. It was ridiculous, but she felt like a child, suddenly unsure of herself. She held the glass firmly, to give her confidence, but it was no use. For some reason he was watching her. She swallowed the brandy quickly. "I think I'd better go to bed early tonight."

"Of course, my dear." Mrs. Thornburn spoke quickly. "But before you go, a little word." She looked across at David, who sat expressionless, glass in hand. "We would like you to reconsider your resignation," she said quietly. "I know it's rather late to be discussing it, but it's so rare that the three of us are together like this, and it seems a good opportunity."

"What my aunt means, Miss Kendrick," said David with a sardonic look at them both, "is that she wants you to say you'll stay. I've told her there's not a cat in hell's chance."

"Really, David!" She turned to Beth. "I'm afraid men have a more forceful way of expressing themselves. You'll have to excuse him."

"It's all right, Mrs. Thornburn," Beth smiled at her.

"I won't see you left without anyone, I promise you that."

"There you are," he said, with a lift of one black eyebrow. "That's your problem solved, Aunt. All you have to do is *pretend* to be trying to get a new secretary. Then Miss Kendrick will stay and stay, because you won't really be trying at all, will you?"

"If you can't talk sensibly, I'm going to bed." Beth helped her up, and handed her her stick, and with a little smile the old lady turned to David, who rose slowly to his feet. "Perhaps we can talk in the morning, David. Goodnight to you both." Beth walked with her to the door, and opened it, and she said quietly: "I can manage, my dear, thank you." Then she went. Beth waited until she vanished up the stairs, then looked round for her bag, which she had put down on the settee. As she went towards it, she heard the doors shut behind her, and turned to see David leaning against them, watching her with a sardonic smile on his face.

She picked up her bag and walked slowly towards him. Something about the very way he stood there should have warned her.

"I'd like to go to bed," Beth said, as pleasantly as possible. "Will you open the doors, please?"

"No. Not until we've had a few words with each other," he answered.

Beth drew herself up to her full height. Very slowly and clearly she said: "You have no right to keep those doors shut. Will you please open them?"

"In a minute. Do you imagine I'm going to seduce you?"

139

"The idea didn't enter my head," she retorted witheringly. "I am tired, however, and I would like to go to bed. Perhaps you've forgotten what happened the last time you argued with me – but you were extremely offensive, and I don't intend to listen to you this time."

"I've no intention of insulting you – at least I don't think so," he answered disarmingly. "I just wanted to tell you that your little scheme didn't work."

"What little scheme?" Beth was beginning to wonder if the brandy had gone to his head.

"Don't look so innocent," he snapped. "I'm not that dim."

"I'm sure you're not," she retorted calmly. "I just don't happen to know what on earth you're talking about."

"Then I'll spell it out. I mean the little plan you and my dear aunt cooked up between you to get me to fall madly in love with you."

"What!" Beth could hardly believe her ears. What was he saying?

"Look," she said. "This gets more ridiculous every minute. How on earth could I think up a plan like that?" It was ludicrous, because he was so painfully near the truth – but in a way he didn't imagine.

"Don't tell me she did it alone." He laughed harshly. "She's cleverer than I thought if she did."

Impatiently Beth walked forward and reached behind his back for the door handle. She found her wrist grasped by his hand. He twisted round and held it loosely before him. "Well, well. I almost believe that she did!" He laughed softly. "And you didn't know!

140

You're such a good actress, it's difficult to know whether you're telling the truth or not."

Beth pulled hard to free the wrist he held so tightly, but it was as if in a steel band. "Patience, little one. Patience." He spoke softly, infuriating her even more.

"Let me go!" she demanded furiously.

"When I've let you in on the joke. You see, my aunt thinks it's about time that I settled down and got married. She doesn't like to see me working away, all alone, so for the past two or three years she's been introducing me at discreet intervals to eligible young females in the hope that I might succumb to their charms sufficiently to relinquish my bachelor status. Alas, it hasn't worked." He released Beth's arm abruptly, and flung it away from him as if it burned him. "And you're the latest, and the last. I must admit she did a good job, picking you, and getting you here to work. You're certainly desirable, you've got brains, and you know how to bat those long lashes to their full effect. You're a bit too young, but we can't have everything perfect, can we?" His voice was mocking and harsh, at the same time, and suddenly sick of it all, Beth put up her hands to her ears.

"Stop it! Stop it! I won't listen," she gasped.

"Yes, you will." With one swift movement he pulled her hands away. "Yes, you will. How do you feel, being part of the cattle market, eh? How do you think *I* feel?"

"You're hateful!" she said. "Hateful! Let go of my hands, you're hurting me!" The words came out in gasping, breathless sobs.

141

"I want to hurt you," he said. "Oh, God, how I want to hurt you." And his mouth came down on hers in a searing, burning, breathless kiss. The next second Beth's hands were released as his arms went round her, hard bands of steel pressing her closely to his body, lifting her almost from the ground. He groaned, his mouth searching for hers, his hands on her back forcing her against him. Then his lips were bruising her, moving from neck to chin, and to mouth again, soft and warm and infinitely to be desired. In a crazy spiral of response that she was unable to resist, Beth found herself, quite against all will and reason, returning the fiery kisses with abandon, and knew that she couldn't help herself.

His breathing was quick and ragged, as if he had been running, and his heart, beating against hers, almost suffocatingly loud. Distantly Beth heard the words, as if from far away: "I want you, oh, how I want you!"

And then, like a slap of cold water, came sanity. Suddenly, shocked icily sober, Beth forced herself to straighten, brace herself against him, and pushed him away. It broke the spell. As he looked at her, face and eyes dark and shadowed, she said shakenly: "That's it. That's all. Now, *let me go*." She could scarcely speak for the thudding of his heart against her ribs, and her legs and arms were weak, too weak to fight him if he touched her again.

Yet he did. Suddenly, before Beth could move, he put his hand up and touched her cheek so gently.

She was rapidly regaining her lost composure. In a

more steady voice, she said: "You seem to make a habit of this, don't you?" Her lips trembled as futile anger rose within her. At that moment she hated him. "And th-thank you for telling me about your aunt's little plot. It's decided me on one thing. I'm going tomorrow. You can type out your own rubbishy scripts after that. In fact, you can b-burn them, for all I care!" Beth felt her voice rising, but she was past worrying about anyone hearing her. "You've treated me like a-a tramp, ever since I came here. Now, at least, I know why you resented me – but that doesn't excuse your trying to take advantage of me. Your behaviour is vile and beastly – and don't bother to apologise, because you've gone too far for that." She took a deep breath. "If you don't get out of my way, I'll hit you!"

"Don't worry," his voice was steadier, almost normal. "I won't stop you. And tomorrow will do fine. In fact, I'll run you to the station myself."

She paused as she was about to pass him. He was almost white with anger, quite suddenly. So he'd run her, would he?

"I'd rather walk," she answered. And she went past him, and up the stairs. She didn't look back. She wouldn't have seen anything if she had. The tears stung her eyes, and blinded her so that she could scarcely see where she was going.

CHAPTER EIGHT

It was with a heavy heart that Beth woke up next morning. She had slept badly, and as she came back to full consciousness, she remembered why. She was leaving Benedict House for the last time in perhaps an hour or so. Leaving it with an unpleasant taste in her mouth, and bitterness in her heart. Overwhelming all else was the knowledge that she would be letting Mrs. Thornburn down. Yet she could not stay. David Benedict, last night, had made that utterly impossible.

She knew the truth at last, and knowing it, could not remain.

Before washing, she packed her suitcase. She intended telling Mrs. Thornburn after breakfast. And if she had to tell her what David had said, perhaps it was better that she should know, instead of vainly hoping to see him settled with a wife.

Beth heard the thud as she dressed herself. It came from Mrs. Thornburn's room next door. For a moment Beth thought she was knocking, and paused in the act of putting on her tights, but it wasn't repeated. She finished dressing, brushed her hair, and was about to open her door when she heard a faint cry – so faint it might have been a cat miaowing in the distance. But a prickle of something ran up her spine, and without thinking why, Beth ran to her door and knocked.

"Mrs. Thornburn, did you call?" It might have been imagination, but. . . .

"Beth?" The answer was faint and unmistakably wavery. "Come in quickly."

She opened the door, then ran forward to where Mrs. Thornburn lay awkwardly on the carpet by the bed. The eiderdown and quilt were half over her and half on the bed, as if she had tried to save herself from falling.

"Stay still," Beth said. "I'll get David." She pushed a pillow under her head, and ran out across the corridor, hammering loudly at David's door as she shouted: "Please come!"

"What the hell —?" The door was wrenched open so abruptly that she almost fell into him. He stood there, a towel slung over his arm, naked from the waist up. In his right hand he held a razor, and judging by the black stubble on his face, had been about to start shaving.

"Mrs. Thornburn's fallen — I heard her call me — please come," Beth said urgently. "I'm frightened to touch her —"

Even as she was speaking, he flung the razor and towel down on a chair, and strode past her, into his aunt's room. Beth followed him, running to keep up with him, to see him kneeling by her side, his face and hair still damp.

"Aunt Lavinia," he said gently, "I'll try and get you back into bed." To Beth, over his shoulder, he called: "Open the bedclothes." She hurried to do his bidding, then waited.

"Can I help you?" she said.

"No. Not yet. Now, do you hurt anywhere — legs or arms?"

145

"No," Mrs. Thornburn whispered. "Oh, David, I'm so sorry to be such a nuisance. I –"

"Ssh!" he stopped her gently. "Don't talk. I don't want to hurt you getting you up, that's all, but I can't leave you in this position until the doctor gets here. So before I move you, I must be sure."

"No – I slipped, that's all. If you could just pull –"

"Save your breath." With infinite care he eased his hands under her back and legs, then with an unbelievable effort of strength, lifted her on to the bed. Beth gently laid the covers over her, bent and picked up the pillow, and eased it beneath her head.

"Shall I get you a cup of tea?" Beth said quietly, aware of David leaving the room.

"Oh, dear, please. If it's no trouble," she began as he walked back, pulling a thin black sweater over his head as he said:

"Beth, phone Dr. Longden, tell him what's happened and that I'm on my way now. I'll be back within fifteen minutes. Leave the tea until he's seen Aunt. Okay?"

He was gone, and Beth immediately went to the phone and began dialling the doctor's number.

She went in the ambulance with Mrs. Thornburn, and David followed in his car. The doctor was doubtful that she had broken any bones, but agreed with David that X-rays were necessary, to be on the safe side. Beth was almost numb with shock, and mingled with it, a feeling of despair. She couldn't go now, today, not until she knew what was wrong. She looked out of the rear window of the gently swaying ambulance at the fol-

lowing car. David couldn't see her, the windows were
of dark glass, but she could see him. He sat easily at
the wheel, seemingly relaxed, yet Beth knew he wasn't.
It was the one thing in his favour, this affection for his
aunt. There was nothing else. He was hard, cold-
blooded and ruthless with everyone else – and especially Beth. Last night he had finally tipped the balance.
Oh, she had been blind, not guessing before. But then
how could she know what had been in his aunt's mind?
Beth looked at her white, lined face on the pillow, and
wanted to cry. She couldn't blame Mrs. Thornburn, nor
apparently could David, so he had taken it out on
Beth. She wondered how many others his aunt intro-
duced him to in the vain hope that he might fall in love.
She remembered her questions when Beth had told her
she was leaving the firm. She had made sure it was all
finished with Alan before asking Beth to work for her.
She should have known, too, that Mrs. Thornburn
couldn't possibly need a full-time secretary. But she
hadn't, and she had walked into the bitter-sweet trap
with ease.

Beth smiled down at Mrs. Thornburn as she squeezed
her hand, and whispered: "All this trouble and fuss."

"It's better to find out if anything's wrong. And
there'll probably be nothing, then you'll be home again."

The old lady tried to smile, but it was an effort, then
she whispered:

"Last night – David – I'm sorry."

Anxiety flared in Beth's eyes, she was unable to hide
it. Had Mrs. Thornburn heard? She must have seen it,
for she said quickly: "Beth, what is it?"

Beth sighed. She didn't want to upset the old lady, but on the other hand a hurt now would prepare her for what she would have to know soon enough. Slowly, choosing her words with care, and making light of it, Beth said: "I'm afraid David is under the impression that you hoped he'd fall in love with me."

Beth smiled as she said it, but she watched Mrs. Thornburn's face, and saw what she'd dreaded to see. Her lip quivered slightly, and she looked almost shame-faced as she said: "I'm not as clever as I thought, am I?"

"You mean —?" Beth stopped. Somehow it made it worse, hearing it from her own lips.

"Oh, forgive me, child. Was he very angry?"

"Angry?" Beth repeated the word, knowing she would never be able to tell her the extent of his anger. Then she nodded. "Yes, he was, a little. And it made it so much worse, feeling as I do. Oh, Mrs. Thornburn, don't look like that, please. But you know I can't stay now. I —" Beth stopped, biting her lip, and Mrs. Thornburn patted her hand.

"I know. I hoped so much —" her voice tailed away, and Beth saw the tears fill her eyes. "I thought — I thought, for a while, that he was —"

"Never," Beth answered. "I'm sorry that your experiment failed. He despises me."

"No," the old lady shook her head feebly. "Not that, never that. Don't say it."

"But it's true. I was going to leave this morning. I'd already packed when I heard you fall. I can take so much, but not any more. I c-can't take any more from him." Beth put her hand to her face, the tears coming freely now. "I must go."

"At least wait – a day or so. Please, Beth, don't leave me when I'm like this. When I'm back at Benedict House, and on my feet, then –"

"Of course I won't." Beth bent and kissed her wrinkled cheek. "Oh, Mrs. Thornburn, he loves you so much, you know. Never think he doesn't. But he's just not interested in anything in life except his writing." She looked out of the window, to see the houses and shops of Buxton. "We'd better cheer up, or they'll keep me in as well." She bent and wiped the old lady's face, so frail and helpless against the pillow, and smiled. "Don't worry – everything will be all right. You'll see." But in her heart was grey despair.

They allowed Beth to stay with Mrs. Thornburn while she had the various X-rays, and as she followed the trolley along yellow corridors, Beth looked back to see David talking to a white-coated doctor in the casualty hall.

Once, while they were taking the X-rays, Beth saw Mrs. Thornburn grimace with pain, and asked her if she was all right.

"Yes, my dear. It's this silly arthritis of mine, that's all. Just playing me up because of all the movement. Don't look so worried, child. I'm as tough as old boots really."

When they had finished, a plump, motherly nurse brought them both a cup of tea as we waited in a small side room.

"Here you are, my dears," she put the cups down

on the locker. "You won't have to wait much longer – though I've an idea they'll want you in overnight."

"But won't they know the results before tomorrow?" Beth asked.

"Yes, but sometimes there's a delayed shock. It's wiser."

Remembering her own, after her own minor fall, Beth nodded. Her heart sank as she realised she would have to go home with David. She would do anything to avoid it, but feared she would have no choice. And so it proved.

A few minutes later, as they finished their tea, the doctor came in, followed by David.

"Well, Mrs. Thornburn," he said, beaming a professional smile at them both, "I think we'll keep you in just a while longer. Mr. Benedict has arranged a room for you, and I'm sure you'll be very comfortable."

"I'm sure I will, Doctor," she answered. "I'll do just as you say." Then, to Beth, "Don't forget, Beth. You will look after Lady Summerfield for me?" She squeezed Beth's hand, who nodded, knowing exactly what Mrs. Thornburn meant.

"I'll look after everything," Beth said. "Can I get you anything from the shops?"

"Nothing, thank you." The old lady looked at the doctor. "May I have a few words with my nephew?"

"Surely. I'm wanted elsewhere, anyway." He grinned at Beth, and went out. Beth made as if to follow, but Mrs. Thornburn spoke: "Wait, Beth. I want you to hear what I have to say to David."

With a sense of foreboding, Beth paused, and half

turned. For the first time ever she saw something approaching anger on the old lady's face as she went on: "This won't take a moment, David. I didn't realise how very foolish I've been these past few years with my little efforts at matchmaking. I'm sorry to have offended you so much, and I can assure you that it won't happen again –"

Beth saw David glance first at her, a smouldering glance, then to his aunt as he moved forward. She went on: "No, you don't need to say anything. Just listen. Beth has told me how she was going to leave this morning – and I've persuaded her to stay. I want you to know that she has never known anything of what was in my mind, and also that she didn't tell me willingly what you had said to her. I made her. And as, for the next few days, she is my guest – no longer my employee, or yours, for that matter – you will treat her with the courtesy you afford to all my guests. Do I have your word that you will?"

He looked just as if she had struck him. Wordlessly he took her hand, then without once looking at Beth, answered: "All right. But please don't worry about it. I didn't want you to know. I wouldn't willingly hurt you for anything, you know that." He looked at Beth then, and she saw the muscles tighten in his cheek, saw the hard directness of his glance, and she looked away, unable to face that merciless stare.

There was nothing more to be said. The long yellow corridors stretched endlessly before them as they went along. Life at Benedict House would be unbearable

151

now; the sooner Mrs. Thornburn was home, the better.

The only words that David said to Beth were: "This way," when she would have gone straight on, instead of turning left. Her heart beat faster. If she refused to go in the car with him, she would be stranded. She knew nothing about a bus service, and had, in any case, left her bag at Benedict House in the confusion.

Beth looked at her watch as they reached his car, parked amongst several others in the large car park at the side of the hospital. It was eleven-thirty, a cold Wednesday morning, with a watery sun trying to struggle through a dull, fuzzy sky. She looked up, wondering if it would snow. It certainly wasn't a normal day for February. There was something odd about the atmosphere, and it matched her mood. David, grim-faced, opened his door, then, leaning over, unlocked the front passenger door and pushed it open.

"Cigarette?" He offered Beth his open case, and she shook her head.

"No, thanks." She knew what he was thinking; that she had waited until they were in the ambulance, and poured out everything of the previous night's events to his aunt. It was no use her telling him otherwise. He would refuse to believe her – and after the Christmas incident when it appeared that she had done the same with Giles, she could hardly blame him. Everything had gone too far for any explanations to do any good. Nothing she said or did would erase the bitterness on his part. And she didn't really care any more.

They drove most of the way home in silence. As they neared the familiar road leading to the house, he said:

"Lady Summerfield is leaving tomorrow. Can you manage her until then?"

For the first time since leaving the hospital, Beth looked at him.

"Manage?" she echoed. "If you mean entertain her, I imagine so. Why?"

He shrugged. "She's difficult. If you want me to take over, I will."

"And leave your work?" She turned indifferently away, and looked out of the window. "Don't bother. I can take her for rides if she gets bored."

"Or to visit Aunt Rose," he added. He was busily intent on steering the large car through the gates, and Beth couldn't see his expression, but she was puzzled. Was he making an effort to be polite, and therefore obeying his aunt's request, or was there a deeper meaning behind his words? She had never seen her so near to anger; perhaps it had shaken him. He had certainly seemed so. Good, Beth thought, savagely, it'll do him good. He was so self-assured, almost arrogant with it, that to see him taken down a peg or two was curiously satisfying. His words of the previous night came back to her suddenly. "I want to hurt you," he had said. Why? Why should it come back to her now, out of the blue? Then she knew. She wanted to hurt him as well, wanted to see him injured, as she had been. In a curious way it had given her satisfaction to see him there, in the hospital, on the wrong end of a tongue-lashing, for a change. Beth turned to watch him as he drove swiftly up the drive. His profile was hard and uncompromising, the stubborn jaw set firm as he watched the road ahead.

153

He gave the impression of a man without mercy or care for anyone. Yet now she knew his Achilles heel, and she felt a little better.

Anne was waiting for them, and flung the door wide open as they stopped in a shower of gravel. David raced up the steps without waiting for Beth.

"What is it?" he demanded.

"It's Lady Summerfield, Mr. Benedict," she answered. "She's very worried about Mrs. Thornburn."

"All right. I'll speak to her. Where is she?"

"In the lounge."

As he strode off he said, over his shoulder: "Bring me coffee and toast, will you, Anne? Miss Kendrick's not breakfasted either."

She looked at Beth. "Phew! What's up with him?"

Beth shook her head. "I can't tell you now. But I packed ready to leave this morning."

"I know," Anne said, as they walked towards the dining room. "I saw your cases when I went in to make the bed. Is that why he's so grim?"

"No. Because Mrs. Thornburn told him off. It's a long story, but the gist of it is this –" and Beth told Anne very briefly, omitting much of what David had done and said – of the events of the previous night, and of this morning.

Anne nodded and looked at her, and perhaps she had seen more in the words than Beth knew, for she smiled a little, then said: "I think you're wrong about him, you know."

"What do you mean?"

"You really don't have any idea, do you? I think –"

154

she spoke very slowly, "– that your loathsome ex-boss is in love with you."

"What!" Beth nearly exploded in disbelieving astonishment.

Anne nodded.. "All right. I know it sounds mad. It even sounds mad to *me*, and it's my idea. But it's just a combination of everything I've ever seen and heard, and what you've told me. And don't forget, I've known him for several years –"

"No, I'm sorry, Anne. I can't accept that. Good heavens, if that's what he behaves like when he loves someone, I'd prefer not to know about it!"

Anne shrugged slightly. "I know. All you say is true. He's a real beast to you, and I'd do what you've done, in your place. But I can't get it out of my head now. I just wish – oh, what's the use? I'll get you something to eat." She gave Beth a wry smile, patted her arm, and went out.

Alone, Beth walked to the window and looked out, Anne's words going round in her mind. She knew the other girl was hopelessly wrong, and yet. . . .

It was so quiet and peaceful outside. A few birds looked in vain for their breakfast crumbs outside the window, and Beth smiled sadly. Soon Mrs. Thornburn would be back to feed them. Until then, she would do it. She opened the window and flung out some toast from the table. A wave of cold air came in and she shivered. It was so damp. A fine thin mist covered the ground further away, giving shrubs and trees a curiously suspended appearance. It was odd; usually these ground mists vanished by noon to give way to warmth and sun,

155

but this was lingering. Beth looked further away, and knew what had bothered her. The hills had vanished completely, as had the furthest trees.

Even as she watched, a roll of mist came sweeping along the grass, swirling and flowing before blending in with the other greyness. She turned quickly as the door opened, and Anne came in with a plate of bacon and eggs.

"Here you are. Not much, but it's lunch in a couple of hours."

"Thanks, Anne. I should have just had toast. I never thought about it." Beth pointed out of the window. "I've never seen a mist like this before."

"No." Anne frowned and put the plate on the table, then came to Beth's side. "Ugh! It's cold when it's like this. You want to shut your bedroom window when you go up, or everything will be covered with a damp sheen." She looked up. "Funny, it's coming over very quickly."

"Does it often happen?"

"Yes, in February especially. They can be quite dangerous for hikers when they come so suddenly. They can trap you just like that!" She snapped her fingers, and Beth shivered, feeling sorry for the sheep and cattle on the hills.

"It was quite clear in Buxton when we left," she said. "And all the way back here."

"That's what I mean. If you walk down the drive now, you won't even be able to see the gateposts until you walk into them."

"That's awful. It's like a thick fog."

Anne laughed. "Except that it's cleaner. That's the

156

only difference. His lordship's with Lady Summerfield. She'll just keep him talking for ages. Feel like rescuing him?"

Beth pulled a face. "No. They deserve each other. I'll eat this and then go and tidy up all my things in the library." She sat down at the table.

With the words, "I'll leave you to it," Anne went out.

It would have been impossible to have taken Lady Summerfield out, even if she had wanted to go. The swirling mist had completely surrounded the house, and isolated it as surely as the snow.

After lunch, a most uncomfortable meal at which she did all the talking, regaling them with accounts of friends of hers who had fallen and broken bones and died, David left them and went back to his study, presumably to write. Beth was left to keep Lady Summerfield amused, a task she would have found difficult at the best of times, but which was almost impossible, feeling so wretched as she did.

It was a relief when Anne brought in tea at four o' clock, and gave Beth a break from listening to Lady Summerfield's life story, and the accounts, all slightly malicious, of the famous people she knew. It was a shame, Beth reflected, as she poured tea into the fine china cups. If only she possessed a sense of humour, how fascinating she would be, for without a doubt she had led an interesting life. Yet everything was coloured by the acid of her nature, and therefore soured.

Beth knew she was a television fan, and tentatively

suggested that she might like to watch the Beverly Hill-
billies, which came on at four-fifteen. She was, to Beth's
delight, agreeable, and breathing a little prayer of
thanks, Beth switched on, waited until the programme
began, and made the excuse that she would have to see
about the dinner.

Safely in the kitchen Beth collapsed in a chair,
watched by Mrs. Macdonald as she prepared the meal.

"Anne's slipped out for a moment," she said. "Giles
phoned."

"Oh, I see. Do you mind if I stay for a little while?
I've left Lady S. watching television, and I'd have started screaming if I'd been in there much longer."

Anne's mother laughed, and Beth saw the likeness to
her daughter in the way she held her head. "Aye," she
answered, "that's understandable. You're welcome to
stay here as long as you like. Pour yourself out some tea,
and there are biscuits in the blue tin."

Beth wandered round the enormous old-fashioned
kitchen, helped herself to biscuits, and studied the high,
blue-papered walls. Even with the modern labour-sav-
ing devices, there was room for improvement, and she
began to realise the amount of money that must be
swallowed up monthly by a house of this size. Mrs. Macdonald was clearly in her element. A portable radio played
quietly in the background as she prepared vegetables at
the huge wooden scrubbed table. Beth sat in an old
rocking chair by the fire and watched her work, envy-
ing her contentment.

The news came on at four-thirty, and she checked
her watch, and stood up regretfully. It really wouldn't

do to leave Lady Summerfield for too long. . . .

"Beth, what's that? Listen!" With a deft hand, Anne's mother leaned over and turned up the volume. Beth stopped the chair from rocking. She too had heard the word, 'Appledore.' They both stood perfectly still as the voice finished the announcement:

". . . are searching for three scouts who failed to report back to their youth hostel this afternoon. They are on an initiative test, and were last seen camping in the hills a few miles from the village. A police spokesman said that visibility in the area is down to a few feet, due to dense mist. In Somerset, a man has been charged with. . . ." She switched it off and looked at Beth. "This is the thing I always fear when the fog comes down." She looked towards the window, and it might have been night outside. All they could see was a grey wall.

"I'd better go and tell Mr. Benedict," she said. "And I hope Anne's not out too long. This'll do her no good." She shook her head. "Those poor boys!"

Beth followed her out, and into the hall, and while Mrs. Macdonald knocked at David's door, she returned to the lounge.

After that everything seemed to happen at once. Lady Summerfield was engrossed in the television, so Beth tiptoed thankfully out again, to bump into Mrs. Macdonald, who had been about to come in.

"Ssh," Beth said, drawing her out again. "She's quite happy."

They stood in the hall, and Anne's mother said, with a nod towards the study, "He was on the phone when I went in, and knows about the missing boys. The doctor

159

phoned to see if we'd seen anything of them here."

Even as she finished speaking, the study door opened and David came out. Without pausing on his way to the stairs, he shouted:

"Get my wellingtons, Mrs. Macdonald, and the thick blue anorak. I'll be down in a minute."

As he vanished, taking the stairs two at a time, Beth said: "He's not going?"

"Yes," the older woman smiled. "He's done this before. Knows these hills like the back of his hand. They always phone here." Beth was surprised to detect a note of pride in her voice, then turned as, distantly, the kitchen door banged and Anne came running in, her hair curling in damp tendrils round her face. She was white, her eyes enormous. Her mother went towards her. "Anne, what is it?" And Anne turned a frightened glance on them both, and bolted upstairs.

Mrs. Macdonald and Beth looked at one another, then Beth said, "Let me go –"

"Yes, do." She passed a hand over her hair, abstractedly. "I must get those wellingtons. Go now, Beth."

Beth ran up the stairs and went full tilt into David, as he turned the corner at the top. For a moment he held her, then stepped back. He had put on a warm sweater, and carried gloves. Frowning, he said: "I've already phoned the hospital to say I can't make it tonight. If I'm not back here in two hours, phone again and ask for Dr. Trent. He's going to tell us the X-ray results. Understand?"

"Yes, Mr. Benedict. I hope you find the boys," she added.

"Thanks." He was already half way down the stairs.

Beth watched him go, with a curiously numb feeling inside her. She had a dreadful sense of foreboding, but she couldn't have put it into words.

Biting her lip, she went along to Anne's room.

"Anne, may I come in?"

A muffled voice answered. "It's not locked."

She opened the door to see Anne sitting on the bed, rubbing her hair with a towel. She looked up, and Beth was relieved to see no sign of tears. But her face was tight with misery.

"Do you want to tell me?" Beth asked softly.

Anne shrugged. "There's not much to tell. Giles and I have had a row, that's all." She gave a wry, twisted smile. "There must be something in the air. I've finished with him." The words came out flat and lifeless, and so calmly that for a moment Beth didn't realise what she'd said. Then she did, and gasped, "Oh, no, Anne!"

"Oh, yes." She shook her head. "I don't know how it started really. Over nothing, I suppose, but one thing led to another, and I – I accused him of being a coward too frightened to tell his mother, and he said something like, he'd tell her when the time was right, and I didn't know how difficult it was – and I said, as far as I can see the time will never be right, and if you think I'm hanging around waiting for ever you're mistaken – and here I am." She rubbed her damp hair vigorously. "It's all over."

"Oh, Anne!" Beth sat down beside her. "You'll make it up, you see."

"No. Not now. Not any more. It's too late. I'm going to leave here – how about me getting a job in London?

Would your mother like a lodger?" Anne tried to smile, and Beth put her arm round her.

"That would be marvellous – but I don't think it's what you really want. Why don't you come downstairs, don't stay brooding up here. Do you know about the three scouts?"

"What?" Anne looked at Beth as if she was mad, so she told the other girl what had happened. It helped to restore the atmosphere to something approaching normal, and Beth managed to persuade Anne to go down with her.

As dinner-time approached, and there was no sign of David, Beth phoned the hospital and learned that Mrs. Thornburn, as Dr. Longden thought, hadn't broken any bones, and would be able to come home the following day, weather permitting. Beth was able to speak to her, and reassured her that everything was going well, and that David, who was very busy, would phone later, if she was still awake. She had no intention of worrying her unnecessarily. Time enough to hear about the scouts when they had been found, and her nephew was safely home. Lady Summerfield insisted on speaking to her friend, so Beth plugged an extension into the lounge, and left her to it.

She was worried. She couldn't help it, although she knew it was stupid to be bothered about a man she couldn't get away from quickly enough. Nevertheless, the heavy, nagging ache persisted throughout dinner, and she ate hardly anything. Mixed with the worry was sadness over Anne. There was nothing anyone could do to help her. Only one person, Giles, could do that, and if he chose not to tell his mother, it was his loss. For Beth was sure he would never meet as fine a girl as Anne again.

All the time, subconsciously, she was waiting for the phone to ring. It was all the greater surprise then, when, as she sat watching television with Lady Summerfield, David walked into the lounge. Before she could stop herself she stood up and went towards him.

"Mr. Benedict! Did you – find them?"

He nodded. "Yes. They made their own way down, and a party near the village reached them first." He peeled off his heavy gloves wearily. "Thank heavens that's over."

It was absurd, but her heart leapt with joy at the sight of him. He was safe! And all the forebodings had been wrong.

"I'll get you some dinner," she said. "I'll go and tell Mrs. Macdonald you're back." He followed her out of the lounge, unzipping the heavy anorak he wore.

"I'll have a bath first," he said, running his fingers through his wet hair. "Make it half an hour. Did you phone the hospital?" His voice was distant, polite and formal, like a stranger's.

"Yes. Mrs. Thornburn hasn't broken anything. I said you might phone later. She can come home tomorrow if the weather clears."

He frowned. "It's thicker than ever. I had to walk back from the village, and leave the car at the doctor's house. It's completely blanketed everything. We'll have to see." He turned and walked towards the stairs, tall, broader-shouldered than ever in the thick heavy coat which he was taking off as he went. And as Beth watched him she wondered if she'd ever love anyone again as she loved him. Loved and hated, at the same time.

Lady Summerfield rarely stayed up late, and soon after ten, announced that she was going to bed. David had gone back to his writing, and the tapping of his typewriter came spasmodically from the study. Beth helped Lady Summerfield to her room, intending to follow not long afterwards herself. She was very tired, but she wanted to have a talk with Anne before she went to bed. She walked slowly downstairs, on her way to see her in the kitchen, when the phone shrilled in the hall, and she picked it up, forgetting that David might answer it in his study.

The agitated voice of Dr. Longden came over clearly, and for a moment Beth thought he was ringing about Mrs. Thornburn as he said: "Miss Kendrick? Get me Mr. Benedict, will you?"

"Just a moment, Doctor." She ran to his study and went in after a brief knock. David looked up from the typewriter with thundery face, but before he could speak, she said: "Dr. Longden wants you."

"Right," he picked up his phone, said: "Hello?" and Beth turned to go out, to put the hall phone down, but was stopped by his next words.

"Oh, my God! Who? Christine Newton?" Beth stopped in her tracks, aware that she was eavesdropping, but physically unable to move as the fear and foreboding rushed back tenfold. Paralysed, she heard his words, not knowing what was happening, yet sensing something so terrible that her heart thudded painfully against her ribs.

"When was this? And they've only just found out? Yes, I'll have a look now, of course – no, I'll ring you back. 'Bye."

He put the phone down and looked up at Beth. She knew her face was white, and with an effort she said: "What's happened?"

"The girl, Christine Newton," he stood up and came round the desk. "She's run away from home."

"Oh, no! Why – how?" she could scarcely whisper.

He shrugged. "I don't know. She was hanging round the village with all the other kids when the crowd was there, then her mother came and hauled her off to bed. They assume that she climbed out of the window of her bedroom – it's over an outhouse – and when her mother went up to see the youngest child she found the bed empty, and her outdoor clothes gone too. Fancy picking tonight of all nights to run away, though! Dear God, what next?"

"No," Beth shook her head. "I think you'll find she's gone to try and find the scouts." She looked up at him. "Don't you see? If she was taken off home before the scouts came down, she'd go to bed thinking they were still lost. Her mother wouldn't think to tell her because she'd expect her to be asleep. What time were they found?"

"About eight."

"There you are. She would – or should – have been asleep by then."

He looked doubtfully at her. "Dr. Longden wants me to look round the gardens. She often comes up here. She could be hiding in the garages." It was obvious that he didn't think much of Beth's theory.

"I'll come with you," she said.

"No, you won't. You'd break your neck in the dark. Phone George and Arthur. They can help." And he strode out without a backward glance.

They said they would be up to the house in two minutes. After she had phoned, Beth went into the lounge, switched off the television and went to the window, drawing back the curtains. She shivered, sick inside, and prayed that Christine would be found, and found soon. She was a child, and so small. The scouts that had been lost were in their teens, adequately clad, and carrying tents and sleeping bags and food. If they hadn't been found, they would have been able to eat, and shelter. But Christine had nothing like that. Only her little legs to carry her, and an old worn anorak and trousers. Beth sat down and put her head in her hands.

The ring at the doorbell roused her, and she got up quickly, expecting the two gardeners. David was running downstairs as she opened it, and Giles walked in. Before either of them could speak, David said: "Good. You can help. Keep your coat on. We're looking for a child from the village." Their voices faded away as they went down the steps, and Anne came up behind Beth.

"Was that —?" she began.

"Giles. Yes. He didn't have a chance to say a word. David grabbed him and took him off to search the grounds. Christine Newton had apparently run away from home, and they think she might be wandering round here."

"Oh, I hope so. I hope they find her." Anne bit her lip. "Poor little thing. It's so cold." Then, as if remembering, she added: "I wonder why G-Giles came?"

"To see you, I think. He looked very determined, only he didn't get a chance to –"

The front door was pushed open and George poked his head in. He was a man of few words. "They gone?" he asked.

"Yes. Try the garage first," Beth suggested.

"Right." He gave a quick salute and vanished, and Beth heard two pairs of boots clattering down the steps.

"I was going to bed," Beth said. "But I can't go now."

"You must, if you're tired. You've had a very hectic day, and there's nothing you can do." Anne looked at her. "They'll find her. They'll be looking from the village too, don't forget."

"Yes, and the mist is worse than ever. It's awful to think about her. I wanted to go and look, but David wouldn't let me." Beth shook her head in despair. "She's so small, little more than a baby."

"Don't, please," Anne begged. "You won't help by upsetting yourself like this. The best thing you can do is wait until they come back and give them a cup of tea."

"You're right. I'll wait in the lounge," she said. "I'll go and get my book first."

"I'll wait with you," Anne gave a small laugh. "His

lordship won't mind – and it's all the same if he does, now I'm leaving."

Beth had to smile. Somehow, having seen Giles' face, she doubted very much if Anne would be going. But she said nothing.

They were back an hour later, just David and Giles. She heard the bell, and Anne went to answer it, then Beth heard Giles say:

"Anne, I want to talk to you. It's very important."

Her answer was lost as the lounge doors opened and David walked in. He looked surprised to see Beth, and as she stood up and asked: "Did you find her?" he shook his head wearily.

"Not a sign. I'll phone."

"I'll get you a cup of tea." She tried to speak naturally, but it was difficult.

"No, wait. I think there's something going on outside. Leave it a moment." He sat down and picked up the phone. Without looking at her, he said: "We're having an extra guest tonight – Giles." Then he was busy dialling, and Beth listened as he spoke. Briefly, without wasting words, he told the doctor that four of them had covered the entire gardens and all outbuildings, and found no trace of Christine. He hung up eventually, and turned to her.

"They've no sign of her either. It's bad. Very bad." He bent and put his hands over his face, and a deep sigh escaped him. "Go and get that tea now, please." As Beth went out, she looked back. He hadn't moved, and he looked exhausted and angry.

There was no sign of Giles or Anne in the hall, and Beth went down to the kitchen, expecting to see them there. But Mrs. Macdonald was alone, clearing everything away for the night.

Beth made the tea and put it on a tray, and as she went out, said: "Oh, by the way, Giles is staying here tonight."

"Yes, I know. Anne's gone to get his room ready. I think he's helping her." There was the slightest suspicion of a smile on her face as she said it, and Beth stopped. "You mean —"

Mrs. Macdonald nodded, eyes shining. "They were talking very seriously. Giles has told his mother!"

"Wow!" Beth's eyes widened. "And she threw him out?"

"From what I can gather, he walked out, and came here. But I dare say we'll find out in the morning, if not before."

"I dare say we will." With those words Beth left her, carrying the tray carefully up the steps, and along through the hall to the lounge where David waited.

She left the tray with him and told him she was going to bed. Something was worrying her. She didn't know what it was, only that she had to think about it. She was in bed, trying vainly to read, when she realised what it was. She sat up abruptly, stunned into the realization of exactly what had been bothering her.

Christine had taken her a walk, only a few days previously, and they had gone to her secret place, barely a mile from Benedict House, a place she often went to alone. What if she had gone there now, hoping to find the scouts, knowing, in her childish way, that the cave would provide shelter for them? A sob rose in Beth's throat as she imagined that small sturdy figure struggling alone, uphill, in the damp, cold darkness, hoping to achieve her ambition to be a mountain rescuer. The utter loneliness she would feel when she arrived, to find nobody there. What then? Would she have the sense to stay, or would she try, exhausted, to find her way back home in the mist?

Beth got out of bed and began to dress herself. She knew where that place was – but would she be able to find it in the utter blankness outside? She didn't know, and there was only one way to find out. She had to do it alone, for it was only an idea, and she had already seen how David treated her theories about Christine. He had already turned out twice, and was angry at the time wasted looking round the gardens.

Beth shivered as she pulled on a warm pair of trousers. Even a man who didn't like children might be expected to have a little sympathy for a lost one, but he had clearly resented having had to turn out that second time.

She slipped on an extra pullover and zipped up her anorak. The bedside clock showed half past twelve. Time for everyone to be in bed. Beth turned round for a last look, to see if she had forgotten anything, then paused on her way out. It would be only common sense to leave a note. She hastily scribbled one and propped it on the pillow. In the unlikely event of her getting lost, Anne would see it in the morning.

All was in darkness as she crept downstairs, and went

towards the front door. Nothing stirred; the only sound was from the grandfather clock ticking slowly in the corner. She reached the door and turned the lock, but it wouldn't open.

Muttering to herself very quietly, she reached up towards the bolt and tried to ease it free, wincing as it grated noisily.

"Damn the thing," she muttered, as it shot open, and she turned the lock again, and eased the door gently open.

Light flooded out as she heard a click, then David's voice, cold and hard, "Where the hell are you going?"

Beth whirled round to see him standing at the lounge door, looking at her with grim puzzlement on his face.

CHAPTER NINE

"I – you frightened me," Beth stammered.

He walked towards her. "Not half as much as you frightened me. Now, I asked you – where are you going?"

Beth tightened her lips, resentment springing up at the arrogance in his voice. Taking a deep breath, she said: "I have an idea where Christine might be. I can't sleep if I don't try it – so I'm going to look."

"Just like that!" he gave a mocking laugh. "You're mad."

"Maybe. But I think of her lying on a cold hillside in this – I can't just do nothing."

"Oh, for heaven's sake," he cut in. "If you set off with that airy-fairy notion in your head, you'll not even get as far as the gates. You need your wits about you on a search. You have to make your eyes, ears, even your nose, work for you in weather like this, and you're trotting off out, just like that." He took the handle and opened the door, letting the damp waves swirl in.

"Look at it! Four of us spent an hour going round the gardens tonight – and we all know them like the backs of our hands – but we couldn't see a bloody thing!" With a gesture of contempt he shut the door. "So how far do you think you'll get? There are twenty or thirty experienced men waiting in the village for morning to come, so that they can start looking again. They know they daren't venture out in this – but you can, of course!"

Beth listened to his angry tirade with a growing dislike inside her. How she hated him at that moment! Strangely, it made her more determined than ever.

"Thank you for your advice," she said icily. "But I still intend to go. I happen to care, you see."

"And I don't?"

"No, I'm sure you don't."

He shrugged. "We won't argue the point. I suggest you go back to bed. There's nothing doing until morning."

"Perhaps you didn't hear me," Beth retorted, trying to keep her voice level. "I'm going to try that one place. Then I'll come back."

"And perhaps you didn't hear me," he answered, steely hard. "I said you're not leaving this house."

"You can't stop me."

"Can't I?" His eyes were slate grey in the bright overhead light, and points of anger danced in them. "I think I can."

Without answering him, Beth reached out to open the door, and his hand shot out and covered hers. He lifted her hand away, then leaned up and shot the bolt. "Now try," he said, and there was mockery about his mouth. It infuriated Beth so intensely that she struck out and slapped his face hard.

"That's the second time that you've hit me," he said, in cold, level tones. "I suggest you don't make a habit of it."

"Then don't be so damned patronising," Beth snapped. "Who the hell do you think you are?"

"At the moment, your host," he replied, infuriatingly. "And I have a duty to my guests, one of which is to see that they don't walk straight into danger – however much they appear to be asking for it."

Beth put her hands to her face in despair. Why were they arguing, wasting time? All she wanted was to find Christine, and the feeling grew stronger every second that she would be at the cave, her secret place.

"Please," Beth looked up at the tall implacable man before her. "Please listen to me. Hear me out, and when I've told you all that's in my mind, if you say I'm wasting my time, I'll abide by it. Will you listen?"

"All right. We can't stand here. Come back into the lounge."

They went in, and as he shut the doors behind them she said:

"I met Christine the other day –" and she told him exactly what had happened, omitting nothing of the conversation, which was still clear in her mind, and of the place Christine had shown her, and where it was, and of the child's desire to be a mountaineer when she grew up and to rescue people. It all came out, and he listened intently, without a single interruption.

When Beth had finished, she looked up exhausted with the effort of remembering everything. And something she saw in his face as he stood there, in front of the dying fire, made her heart lift.

He looked steadily at her. In a tone quite unlike any she had ever heard him use, he said: "I think you have something. I only wish you'd told me sooner."

"But I only thought about it after I got into bed. It was at the back of my mind all evening, but I didn't know what it was."

David reached over to the coffee table and passed her a notebook. "Can you draw a rough sketch of where this place is?"

Beth nodded. "Yes, I'm sure I can."

"Then do it. I'll get us a drink. We're going to need one."

He handed her a glass of brandy and took the sketch from her. Sipping his own, he looked at the drawing from several angles, then at her. "All right. I've got a damned good idea where this is. I'll come with you."

"You'll –" Beth nearly choked on the brandy, and gasped before managing to finish. "*You* will? But I don't –"

"It's me or nothing," he said drily. "Take your choice. Drink up, then we'll go and change."

"But I am changed – I mean –" she looked down at herself.

"Go and get an extra sweater on. I'll do the same. If – when – we find her, we'll put them on her. She'll need them, and they'll be warm from our bodies." He crossed to the drinks cupboard, and lifted out a small metal flask, which he shook. "That'll do. Come on, I'll get the wellingtons."

Ten minutes later they stood outside the front door. She felt clumsy, wearing three pullovers, and wellingtons, but the thought that they would be of practical use was enough to make her glad.

The black night was impenetrable. Behind them the

house, in darkness, was already invisible. Beth felt as if she was breathing under water, a frightened sensation, but one she was to get used to in the next few minutes. They walked along the drive, the only sounds the faint crunch of gravel underfoot, and their breathing.

"Don't waste your breath in unnecessary talk," David had warned her before they left the warmth and safety of the house. "And take shallow breaths." And he had handed her a scarf. She wore it over the bottom half of her face, as he did his, and they would have looked, to any passer-by, like two bank robbers. But there was no one to pass by, there was nobody at all except them and a child they needed to find.

Beth was completely lost, and they were still in the grounds of the house, on the path to the gate. With sinking heart she realised that David had been completely right. If she had ventured out alone, she would have been as surely lost as Christine, and no use to her at all.

When they reached the high gateposts, and stopped for a moment to take their bearings, Beth said: "I owe you an apology. I'd never have made it alone."

She couldn't see his face for the scarf muffling it, but he shook his head, and said: "You've got guts, anyway. You were going to try. Come on. It's this way, isn't it?" They began walking along the road outside, and he went on: "If you're in any doubt, stop me. I'm going by your map, as I see it, but we've got to be in agreement, okay?"

She nodded her understanding, and they went on. Soon Beth got an uneasy feeling, and touched his arm. "Wait."

"What is it?"

"I think – it was near here that we turned off the road, but I can't be sure exactly –"

"Did you climb over a stone wall, or a stile, or a gate?"

She cast her mind back, trying to see, to remember exactly what they had done, then in sudden relief as memory came, she clutched his arm. "That's it! It was a stile – only a funny one, like a little narrow gate that only one person could get through at a time. I remember because I thought as I went through that animals wouldn't be clever enough to push and turn at the right moment. . . ."

"Hold it," he said. "I've got it. Good girl!"

It was so ridiculous, the warm glow that came with his words, and the approving pat on her arm. They set off, moving more slowly now, close by the ditch at the side of the road, their eyes straining in the effort. And then – "That's it." He stopped, and Beth saw the familiar little gate before them. And it was at that moment that she knew they would find the cave, the secret place.

The climbing was difficult. It was rough underfoot, and the ground was damp, so that their wellingtons squelched and slithered on hummocks of grass. Beth was trying not to take deep breaths, but had to, and a sudden pain in her side made her gasp and pause.

"What is it?" David stopped beside her.

"Nothing, just a stitch," she answered, her voice hoarse.

"Here, have a drink of this," he pulled out the flask from his anorak pocket, unscrewed the top, and poured some liquid into it.

She sipped the brandy, feeling immediately warmer as the golden fire coursed into her stomach. "Oh, that's better!"

"Good." Beth couldn't see his face, but she knew that he was smiling, and suddenly he peeled off his left glove and stuffed it into his pocket. "Take your right glove off," he said, in a tone that brooked no refusal. Puzzled, she did so, and then felt his warm strong hand clasp hers. "Come on, we'll walk like this. It's safer for us both, now that we're climbing, and I can help you if you're flagging. Are we going in the right direction?"

So confused was she by his action that for a moment Beth couldn't answer. His hand was so warm, and strong, and comforting – and more. The very touch made her heart beat suffocatingly loud. If only he knew what he'd done! And yet to him it was just a gesture of companionship in their mutual struggle up the hill. And a temporary truce, that was all. Yet suddenly it didn't matter, nothing mattered, because everything was unreal, dreamlike. The mist, suspending everything in a strange cold world of unreality, seemed to have taken over, and transformed them into something quite different. . . .

"Yes," Beth realised that he was waiting for an answer. "It's a lot higher, and in a minute we should come to a wall. The bit we climbed over was collapsed, with several huge flat stones on the ground."

He squeezed her hand reassuringly. "That's it. Try and remember these little things, they'll help us keep our bearings. Right, one wall coming up. Fingers crossed." And with that they set off, and the going was suddenly easier. Dark grey mist swirling round them at every step, the ground horribly uneven, and steeply uphill, yet she was filled with an exhilarating sense of well-being.

That was dashed the next moment when they came to a high stone wall. It loomed up on them suddenly. They stopped. He looked at Beth.

"Is this it?" he asked quietly.

"I don't know – it – the one we climbed was much lower," she answered hesitantly.

"Don't sound so worried." Again the comforting pressure of his hand on hers. Just for a moment, but it was enough.

"We'll go along it to the left, as far as we can, then come back and go to the right," he said. "And so that we know exactly where we started from, I'll put a marker on the wall." He dug into his pocket and produced a hanky, and wedged it firmly on the top of the wall with a small pebble.

"That'll do. It'll help on the way home too."

Half an hour later they found the gap in the wall, but only after a fruitless journey to the left, and back again. Beth knelt and felt the ground round them as they reached the gap. "Yes, this is it. I remember there was some dried-up heather by one of the stones, and I can just feel it."

David knelt beside her. "Are you tired?" he asked. "Do you want a rest?"

"No. Not until we find her."

"Come on." He stood up and pulled her to her feet. "Let's go."

Hand in hand they went on, ever upwards, and a pulse of excitement beat in Beth's throat. They were nearly there, and soon they would know. A sob rose in her throat. What if Christine wasn't there?

"Beth? What is it?" She sensed anxiety in his tone.

"I just thought – if she wasn't there," she said.

"Then don't. Don't even think it. Wait and see."

"Yes." Beth accepted the rebuke, and added, "Thank you for coming. I'd have been frightened on my own, I realise that."

"And you're not now?"

"Not with you, no."

He stopped abruptly, forcing her to do the same. "That's just about the nicest thing you've ever said to me." And there was no sarcasm in his voice. Then, as if realising a moment of weakness, he pulled her. "Come on, we'll never get there if we stand talking."

Suddenly the ground became very familiar, flat, and much smoother. Beth tightened her grip on his hand. "We're nearly there. Up to the right, I think – yes – oh, yes!" She saw the huge looming shadow of the higher slope in front of them swimming out of the mist, and she pulled him, trying to run.

"Don't rush," he held her back, steadying her pace. "We'll be there in a minute. Beth?"

"Yes?"

"We'll know, one way or another, very soon."

"Yes." Her heartbeats were suffocatingly loud, and she felt the gentle pressure of his hand, as he added quietly: "And I hope that you're right."

"So do I."

Beth bent and crouched down as they reached the towering rocks that formed the mouth of the cave. All was blackness within, and so quiet, that as he crouched beside her, she whispered: "She's not –"

A beam of light pierced the inky blackness before them as he switched on his torch. In its yellow path a bundle was revealed, a pathetic blue bundle, lying on the floor of the cave. Beth drew in her breath sharply. "It's –" as she bent forward to crawl in, he stopped her.

"No, I'll go. Hold the torch." And very slowly he eased himself forward towards the inert child. And as his hand went underneath that grubby blue anorak, Beth knew why he had wanted to go first, and breathed a silent prayer. The tears pricked her eyes, blurring the cave walls and the shadows into one swimming mass of grey.

Then he turned, pulling down the scarf from his face as he said: "She's cold, but her heart's beating well. Come here."

A moment later she was by Christine's side, blinking desperately at the tears. David was already taking his coat off, and pulling his thick sweater over his head.

"Ease her up," he commanded, and as she did so, he pulled his sweater over her. It covered her from neck to toe, and he looked at Beth. "Take yours off as well. I'll try and rouse her."

He lifted the unconscious child into a sitting position and began gently rubbing her cheeks, repeating: "Wake up, Christine," over and over patiently. Then he put

Beth's jumper over her legs and pulled it up over her shoulders, upside down, all the while cradling her in his arms. Beth watched, wanting to help but knowing instinctively that what he was doing was best.

Suddenly a faint murmur came, a sleepy mumble from the child, but it was enough. Beth knelt beside her and looked at him, and grinned.

"Let's get her awake sufficiently to give her some brandy. Talk to her, Beth."

She touched the child's white face, and said: "Christine, it's me, Beth. Do you remember our walk? Did you come looking for the scouts, Christine?" Gently she kissed the child's cheek, then put her own against it, willing warmth and life into the pitiful little body.

"Mummy?" a sleepy murmur, and her eyes fluttered open as Beth took her from David and cradled her in her arms.

"No, love, it's me, Beth. You remember?" She could scarcely speak for the aching lump in her throat. Christine was going to be all right, Beth knew it in her heart, and could have wept for joy.

As Beth held her, David drew the flask out and poured some brandy into the cap. He put it to her lips. "Come on, there's a good girl. Have a drink of this."

Christine took a tentative sip, then pulled a violent face, and her muffled hand came up to push David's away.

"Ugh, nasty medicine," she grumbled, looking at Beth.

"It's to do you good," David said firmly.

"Don't want it," was the prompt reply. He grinned

and got lithely to his feet, replacing the cap. "She knows best." He bent and pulled them both up. "All right, Beth. I'll carry her now. Pick up her things."

Beth bent to the floor of the cave and carefully lifted a small string bag from beside where she had lain. A bar of chocolate fell out, and in the bag was a teddy bear and a small blanket. Beth held them up. "Look," she said. "She brought these."

David and Beth looked at one another over the sleepy child in his arms, and as their eyes met, Beth saw in his something that moved her immensely. It was a deep compassion, a tenderness she wouldn't have thought existed. He said softly: "She came here alone, just like that. Poor little kid!"

"Yes. I apologise. I accused you of not caring, before. I'm sorry." Beth couldn't help herself.

"I care. I care very much," he answered softly, and he smiled.

Two hours later they were sitting on a settee at Dr. Longden's house, drinking hot chicken broth from beakers, while Mrs. Longden, in a voluminous blue dressing gown, fussed round them.

Christine was in a warm bed in the next room, being examined by the doctor while her mother sat at the bedside, red-eyed from weeping, and almost hysterical in her gratitude.

The lights dipped and swayed, and Beth felt David take the beaker from her. "Careful, you nearly spilt it."

"Yes. Sorry." Beth knew she was mumbling, but she

couldn't help it. All her body craved was sleep, oodles of sleep, in a lovely warm bed, and. . . .

She opened her eyes to find herself sitting in a car, going extremely slowly down a mist-shrouded road. David's voice came faintly, from miles away. "Go back to sleep. We're going home."

Home. He meant Benedict House, but he'd said home. It sounded so very right. So very right. With a little sigh, she closed her eyes again.

She woke up as the car stopped in front of the house, and looked around her in amazement. The mist was as thick as ever, and it was still night. Yet she felt as refreshed as if she had slept for hours, but was astonished to see, as she looked at the dashboard clock, that only an hour had passed since they had been at the doctor's.

"You drove home in this?" she said, as they got out and crept quietly up the steps.

"Yes. We could have stayed there the night, but – well," he shrugged, "I prefer my own bed. Don't you?"

"Yes. I imagine you're more tired than me," Beth answered, as she watched him fitting the key in the lock. "I have at least had a sleep."

"I can manage with very little, if I have to," he swung the door open and they went into the darkened hall. "Go into the lounge. I need a drink. Will you have one?"

"Yes. Just a drop, to celebrate." She bent and eased off the heavy wellingtons. "Ah, that's better!"

Inside the lounge, watching him get the drinks, she

184

said: "Will she be all right?"

"Christine? Yes. She's a sturdy child. A day in bed, and she'll be as right as rain." He looked up from the bottle he held. "Thanks to you."

"No," Beth shook her head. "I'd never have done it alone. I knew that soon after we set out. I would have been hopelessly lost."

He handed her a glass, then raised his own. "Then here's to both of us."

They drank, and suddenly faintly embarrassed, she said: "Have you a cigarette?"

"Certainly." He reached into a pocket of his discarded anorak, and brought them out. "Let me help you off with your coat," he said. "You'll be boiling."

"Yes, thank you." Beth put her glass down on the table and stood up. He reached out and began to help her off with her anorak. She was half turned away from him as he did so. Then, as if in slow motion, she put her arms slightly back, because that made it easier to get off, and she felt his hands tugging at the sleeves, pulling them, and half turned to ease it off fully. And his hands came up and round to take the jacket off from the front, but somehow they kept on coming round, and didn't stop until they were around her. And then his mouth was on hers, and this time it was different from anything that had ever happened before. This kiss was so tender, and full of love that Beth responded like a flower to the sun. They seemed to be revolving gently round until she opened her eyes and realised it was just the effect he had on her. She had gone so dizzy that she had to hold on to him to keep from falling. He groaned, and kissed her again, and that one was better still. Beth pushed her head away sufficiently to murmur:

"Please stop this. You mustn't, you know."

"No, I know. But I've suffered long enough. I don't care any more. I love you, Beth Kendrick."

"What?" she murmured faintly, nuzzling his ear. "You're mad."

"I know, but what the hell. Come here, woman." And that was that, for at least half an hour.

"What did you say?" she pushed him away suddenly, as the meaning of his words sank in.

"I said I love you, dammit!" David made a determined effort to bury his face in her hair again, but she stopped him, with difficulty. They had somehow got on to the settee, though Beth didn't remember how, but it seemed as good a place as any to be, especially as her legs had turned to jelly.

"You can't. You hate me," she said flatly, pushing him away. "You treat me like – like something awful. I'm the one who's mad, letting you kiss me like this. How dare you!"

"Don't," he begged. "Don't start that again. I've taken all a man can stand. I can't go on any more – and I can't let you escape. I've been such a fool," he gave a groan and buried his head in his hands. "Say you don't hate me, Beth. Please say it."

"Oh, David," she laid her hand gently on the back of his head, "if only you knew!"

He looked up slowly. "You called me David. That's the first time you've ever done that, you know. Say it again, please."

186

"David, David. Don't you know when a woman loves you?"

His face grew sad. "There's no need to joke."

"I'm not joking, you idiot. Oh, love!" she put her arms round him joyously as all the tiny pieces of jigsaw fell into place, and she knew at last what she should have known all along. "My love, don't you see? I love you too. Have done for so long, but you were so hard and cruel, like a stranger, that I knew – or thought I did – that you despised me."

He gently eased his arm more securely round her, and with his fingers, traced a line along her chin. "Yes, I was a brute, wasn't I? There was a reason for it. God, what an absolute swine I must have been to you!" He shook his head. "How did you put up with me?"

"I gave up, yesterday, remember?" Beth answered simply.

"So you did. And I'd have let you go, because –" he stopped, and cupped her face in his hands. "Because I'm a stubborn, stupid man who doesn't know what's good for him. Oh, my darling, to think that I might have lost you –"

"But why?" Beth asked. "Why did you –"

He silenced her with a tender kiss. "Because – oh, for so many reasons that seem false, now that I know. It was at the cave, seeing you tending to Christine, loving her to bring her back to life, that I had my eyes truly opened at last, and I knew I could never let you go." He leaned back and eased her more comfortably into the curve of his arm, and then, in that utter stillness of the night, he began talking.

"You remember our first meeting here, that day in the garage? I was strongly attracted to you then, seeing you there, your hair loose, your cheeks pink with the cold air. And I knew you were the girl I'd seen with Alan coming out of the cottage in Sussex that weekend, a few weeks before. Alan's got quite a reputation, and to be frank, I thought you were just another of his birds –" he put a finger to her lips "– no, don't say anything. I know nothing happened there, but meeting you so suddenly, putting two and two together, knowing Aunt Lavinia's habit of pushing eligible girls at me with gay abandon – I set up an automatic barrier, which was reinforced when I saw how friendly you and Giles were. Okay, I said to myself, she's a flirt – and I'd no intention of letting my scalp go on your belt, especially as Aunt Lavinia was hovering in the background, hoping quietly that I'd fall in love with you." He laughed softly. "The irony is that I did just that – and I fought like hell, believe me. It was agony, working with you every day, trying not to grab hold of you every time you brushed past me, fighting a natural, basic desire to make love to you. So I buried myself in work, and became more grouchy than ever. Then, at Christmas, you remember?" Beth nodded.

"I'd never behaved to any woman like that before, believe me. Then, when all was well, you came out with that remark, which made it seem you'd gone straight to Giles. God forgive me," he said bitterly, "I thought you'd been lying, all you'd said –"

"It was an accident," Beth interrupted. "I'd only told him by chance. I –"

188

"Don't you think I don't know that? Oh, my love! I know you. You couldn't be a cheat, you're incapable of deceit. You're perfect, precious, and I've trampled all over you in the most brutal way possible. There's another thing. I'm thirteen years older than you. My father was that much older than my mother, and their marriage ended disastrously. So I fought this attraction, because of all these things, fought the absurd joy the sight of you gave me. Oh, darling, I've been lost all my life, looking for something, I knew not what – until I met you – and then I so nearly destroyed it all, because of my own stupidity." His voice was shaking.

"Oh, David, to think I'd have gone from here! And you'd have let me go, just like that?"

"No," he said quietly. "For a while, yes, because I thought you didn't know your own mind. Alan, then Giles, what else was I to think? You have to have time, at twenty, to choose. But it couldn't have ended there, it couldn't have. I knew I'd see you again. Knew I'd have to find you – but I don't need to. You're here." He took her hand and placed it on his heart. "That's where you belong, and will stay, for ever."

Beth smiled, and snuggled contentedly down beside him. And as the room gradually lightened, and morning came, bringing with it a lessening of the mist, they sat there talking, planning, all need for sleep gone, happy beyond words to be together, at last knowing the truth, and with it, a deep and lasting contentment. Beth wouldn't leave Benedict House again. All the dreams she had had, of it being home, had come true, as had all the dreams about the man she loved, David Benedict.

THE
OMNIBUS
Is Here!

A GREAT NEW IDEA
From HARLEQUIN

OMNIBUS — The 3 in 1 HARLEQUIN
only $1.50 per volume

Here is a great new exciting idea from Harlequin. THREE GREAT ROMANCES — complete and unabridged — BY THE SAME AUTHOR — in one deluxe paperback volume — for the unbelievably low price of only $1.50 per volume.

To introduce the Omnibus we have chosen some of the finest works of four world-famous authors....

> JEAN S. MacLEOD
> ELEANOR FARNES
> ESSIE SUMMERS
> MARY BURCHELL

.... and reprinted them in the 3 in 1 Omnibus. Almost 600 pages of pure entertainment for just $1.50 each. A TRULY "JUMBO" READ!

The first four Harlequin Omnibus volumes are now available. The following pages list the exciting novels by each author.

Climb aboard the Harlequin Omnibus now! The coupon below is provided for your convenience in ordering.

HARLEQUIN OMNIBUS

☐ **JEAN S. MacLEOD**

    The Wolf Of Heimra   (#990)
    Summer Island   (#1314)
    Slave Of The Wind   (#1339)

    $1.50

☐ **ELEANOR FARNES**

    The Red Cliffs   (#1335)
    The Flight Of The Swan   (#1280)
    Sister Of The Housemaster   (#975)

    $1.50

☐ **MARY BURCHELL**

    A Home For Joy   (#1330)
    Ward Of Lucifer   (#1165)
    The Broken Wing   (#1100)

    $1.50

☐ **ESSIE SUMMERS**

    Bride In Flight   (#933)
    Meet On My Ground   (#1326)
    Postscript To Yesterday   (#1119)

    $1.50

THE 3 IN 1 VOLUME —
EACH VOLUME BY THE SAME AUTHOR
    — ONLY $1.50 EACH